WELL-DESERVED A...

THE NEAL POLLACK ...
AMERICAN LITERATURE

"One of the greatest satires of authorial vanity to come along since the actual career of Norman Mailer."

—Will Blythe, *Rolling Stone*

"Every fatuous magazine writer who's even contemplating boarding a freighter, befriending a working-class black woman, dropping a celebrity name, or subjecting us to his narcissistic maunderings about life, death, identity, and Cuban hookers should shrivel into a little gray lump at the very sight of this book."

—Laura Miller, Salon.com

"The completely fictional work of a well-studied satirist. . . . Plus he looks great in fatigues."

—*Entertainment Weekly*

"The joke proves surprisingly durable. . . . Pollack forever soils the genre of literary journalism."

—Jack Shafer, *New York Times Book Review*

"Graceful and redemptive . . . hypnotic . . . joyous and heart-wrenching . . . harmonious . . . inventive, bawdy, and tremendous . . . eccentric and larger than life . . . gripping . . . deeply moving . . . *con brio* and *amore,* Pollack writes with gusto and panache . . . excellent . . . seamless."

—*Adjectival Ellipsis Quarterly*

"An extraordinarily inventive bag of riches that encompasses all of human history! An exhilarating breath of air that can only be inhaled in one sitting! One of the finest books ever written! A magical joyride that will have you on the edge of your seat! I could not stop laughing!"

—David Manning, *Ridgefield Press*

"Not terrible at all."

—Judith Shulevitz, also in *New York Times Book Review*

CSW Film Systems, Inc.

About the Author

NEAL POLLACK, the author of this bestselling book, is the moon-bewildering apogee of male beauty in the visible universe, and possibly beyond. Let his picture guide your thoughts and your hand. Do not be ashamed of what it makes you do. The human body is a treasure, and the feelings it feels are blessed. Neal endorses your actions. He lives in Philadelphia.

THE
NEAL POLLACK
ANTHOLOGY
OF AMERICAN
LITERATURE

The Collected Writings of Neal Pollack

NEAL POLLACK

Perennial

An Imprint of HarperCollins*Publishers*

The photographs appearing in the photographic insert following page 99, courtesy of Nathan Mandell.

A hardcover edition of this book, in somewhat different form, was published in 2000 by McSweeney's Books.

HarperCollins books may be purchased for educational, business, or sales promotional use. For information please write: Special Markets Department, HarperCollins Publishers Inc., 10 East 53rd Street, New York, NY 10022.

First Perennial edition published 2002.

Library of Congress Cataloging-in-Publication Data

Pollack, Neal.
  The Neal Pollack anthology of American literature / Neal Pollack.—
1st Perennial ed.
    p. cm.
  Includes bibliographical references.
  ISBN 0-06-000453-3
  1. Authorship—Humor. 2. American literature—Humor. I. Title.
PN6231.A77 P65 2001
814'.6—dc21   2001036952

02 03 04 05 06 ❖/RRD 10 9 8 7 6 5 4 3 2 1

CONTENTS

ACKNOWLEDGMENTS ix

PUBLISHING NOTES xi

PREFACE TO THE PERENNIAL EDITION:
CONFESSIONS OF A HARD-CORE HEROIN USER xiii

INTRODUCTION xv

CHRONOLOGY xix

THE ALBANIA OF MY EXISTENCE 1

DATELINE: COLOMBIA 3

I AM FRIENDS WITH A WORKING-CLASS BLACK WOMAN 7

IT IS EASY TO TAKE A LOVER IN CUBA 13

MEMORIES OF TIMES SQUARE 19

PORTRAIT OF AN ANDALUSIAN
HORSE TRAINER 23

THE BURDEN OF INTERNET CELEBRITY 27

INTERLUDE: *THE OPRAH WINFREY SHOW*, MARCH 15, 1996 31

MY WEEK AT SEA 37

BLURBS [AND FOOTNOTE TO BLURBS] 43

LETTER FROM PARIS 47

A COUNTRY HOUSE IN THE COUNTRY 51

I Have Slept with Five Hundred Women   55

Introduction to the New Slavery
   [Footnote: The Review, Etc.]   57

Stand by John   67

A Doctor Cannot Save Your Life   71

An Interview with My Sister, Who Is a Lesbian   75

Lake Minnesota Days   81

To Search for the Celtic Tiger   85

The Rise and Fall of the New Economy   91

Interlude: The Pollack-Wilson Letters   95

Teenagers: The Enemy Within
   [Footnote: About Tennis]   101

Interlude: *The Paris Review* Interview, June 27, 1976   117

The Coitus Chronicles: A Trilogy in Three Acts   125

The Subcomandante Rides at Dawn   137

One Writer's Routine   149

Why Am I So Handsome?   153

The First Annual New York University Neal Pollack
   Chair in American Literature Lecture   163

Witness for the Revolution   167

Secrets of the Mystery Jew   175

Coda: A Review of My Contemporaries   183

Breaking News: One Against the Taliban   189

study guide   201

ACKNOWLEDGMENTS

I didn't really need much help in putting this tome together. Nevertheless, it would be rude of me to ignore all the people whom I have lent my guest house to, picked up at the airport, and prepared breakfast for over the years. I am grateful to all of you, particularly to Bishop Desmond Tutu; Bjork; Ashleigh Banfield; Allen Iverson (The Answer); the late Joey Ramone, my friend and mentor in all things punk; the late Dian Fossey; and my dear friend and admiral John Poindexter. Also, I wish to pay special consideration to my parents, whose bulging fortune, unsoiled genes, and Italianate country villa allowed me the time and meditative rest necessary in my early years so I could blossom into the master I am today.

Also, I must greet the people, too many, really, some of whom I hate now, who gave me the following places to write:

The winery in Umbria, the three-story beach house in Costa Rica, the cashier's booth at the Flamingo Hotel, Las Vegas, the outhouse in suburban Fairbanks, the guest lounge at the *Today* show, the infested chair in the deserted Chicago junkyard, the room with the view, the basement of the federal prison in Idaho, the vanishing rain forest of Nigeria, Pieter's Groovy Hash Hut in Amsterdam, the linen closet at the headquarters of *Martha Stewart Living,* the gingerbread house in the forest, the thin sliver of balcony overlooking the pool during Spring Break '92, the old stone farmhouse in Vermont where several classics majors brutally murdered a classmate who couldn't keep his mouth shut, somewhere beyond the sea, and, strangest of all, my apartment in Brooklyn.

I suppose I should also recognize my enthusiastic and brilliant agent, Rebecca Kurson, as well as my former agent, John Hodgman, who is incessantly and, I might add, unnecessarily trying to kill me. Then there's my editor, David Hirshey. He saved this book from eventual extinction, assisted by Jeff Kellogg, who doesn't sleep enough. Also thanks to Jennifer Hart for helping this irascible curmudgeon seem lovable to his younger readers, Lizz Pawlson for booking me in the nicest hotels possible given the obscene parsimony of my corporate masters, and Carrie Kania, of HarperAudio, for making the band. Together, we fooled all the people, all the time.

Thanks also to Danny Eggleston, an up-and-coming but almost totally worthless young writer, and the various other poorly paid drones from the McSweeney's literary collective who have toiled on my behalf, including Matt Fogel, Ted Thompson, Diane Vadino, Windsor Beaver, Sarah Min, Julie Wright, Jessica Reik, and Laurence Lowe. Todd Pruzan, as always, provides ballast and an uncomfortable sofa bed. To my home city of Philadelphia, I say hello, but I curse your fucking stupid self-employment tax, goddammit. And I want to give a "shout out" to my current wife, Regina, for blowing me in the hot tub, all the time, and forever more. Babe, this book is for you.

PUBLISHING NOTES

Dateline: Colombia" previously appeared in *Harper's* as "I Want a New Drug War"; "The Albania of My Existence" previously appeared in *GQ* as "This Albanian Life"; "I Am Friends with a Working-Class Black Woman" previously appeared in the *New York Times Magazine* as "Grumble in the Bronx"; "It Is Easy to Take a Lover in Cuba" previously appeared in *The Atlantic Monthly* as "The Buena Vista Anti-Social Club"; "Memories of Times Square" previously appeared in *New York* as "Crouching Mayor, Hidden Strippers"; "Portrait of an Andalusian Horse Trainer" previously appeared in the *Saturday Evening Post* as "Spain in the Ass"; "My Week at Sea" previously appeared in *Outside* as "Sail of the Century"; "The Burden of Internet Celebrity" previously appeared in *Fast Company* as "Come Online Eileen"; "Letter from Paris" previously appeared in *Slate* as "All He Wants to Do Is France"; "A Country House in the Country" previously appeared in *Food & Wine* as "Fabulous Rooftop Brunch for Six"; "Introduction to the New Slavery" previously appeared in *Cigar Aficionado* as "At Home with Danny DeVito"; "Stand by John" previously appeared in *Newsweek* as "McCain and Able"; "A Doctor Cannot Save Your Life" previously appeared in *Ellery Queen Mystery Magazine* as "Prescription for Murder"; "An Interview with My Sister, Who Is a Lesbian" previously appeared in *The Weekly Standard* as "Gay for a Day"; "Lake Minnesota Days" was originally performed on National Public Radio's *A Hairy Prom Companion;* "To Search for the Celtic Tiger" previously appeared in *Rolling Stone* as "Nothing Compares 2 Ireland"; "The Rise and Fall of the New Economy" previously appeared in *Business 2.0* as "Headline TK"; "Teenagers: The Enemy Within" previously appeared in the *Dallas Morning News* as "Zero Tolerance: How Much Is Too Much?"; "The Coitus Chronicles" previously appeared in *The Source* as "Outkast Gets Stanky"; "The Subcomandante Rides at Dawn" previously appeared in *The Progressive* as "Down Mexico Way"; "Why Am I So Handsome?" previously appeared in *Esquire* as "The Lost Art of Driving Drunk"; "Witness for the Revolution" previously appeared in *Z Magazine* as "Why Ralph Nader Will Be Our Next President"; "Secrets of the Mystery Jew" previously appeared in *Granta* as "Mysteries of the Secret Jew," in *The New Yorker* as "Mysterious Secretions of the Jew," and in *Road & Track* as "Jeff Gordon's Wild Ride." All pieces appear courtesy of the author, who, as he writes, gazes winsomely at the rushing Ligurian surf, remembering the cheetahlike form of Wally Trumbull, his former roommate at Exeter. Have patience, Wally dear! Do not abandon your Valhalla in the air! I am coming hence, for you are my one love and my eternal passion.

PREFACE TO THE PERENNIAL EDITION: CONFESSIONS OF A HARD-CORE HEROIN USER

Can you hear me? Can you hear me late at night, Doris, when the needle is between my toes and the blood spills across my rolled-up socks, pools of evidence on shredded, stinky cotton? Can you tell me where it's gone, the future and the past, my life as a corporate litigator, an investigative journalist, a children's-toy manufacturer? In the last corner, the final mote of my conscious brain, I can still remember what it was like. I had a change of clothes, a cavalcade of prostitutes who would service me at will, and a lawn. Often, I was at parties, important parties at famous restaurants, and inside I was laughing at the people who were not like me, the people who went to work sober and happy, and went home the same calendar day without once—once!—getting high. I made so much money, and I spent it all on smack, hard, dark smack the color of night. Well, I spent some of it on groceries, too, and I also bought some grout for the bathtub, but mostly on smack. Where has it gone, Doris? What hideous demon has propped open my eyelids with his pitchfork and scraped the inside of my mouth with a cheese grater?

The guy in the bed next to me keeps trying to hit my balls with a hammer. I feel his hot breath on my face all the time. It smells like Ital-

ian beef, and I know that rehab is hell. Was it really only twenty years ago that I was freebasing at Ginsberg's place in the Village, five years ago that my veins exploded while I was interviewing Madeleine Albright, covering her face in viscous plasma, two years ago that I was shooting horse on the set of Walker, Texas Ranger? *Was it really only last week that the cops raided that crack house and found me cooking up a spoonful of fresh ground pepper? I had a wife once, I think, but she got sick of the drugs and traded me to Atlanta for Dikembe Mutombo. Or was I dreaming that, too? But I will get better, Doris, whoever you are. This confession is proof that I can come through, that I can still write, that smack can nibble, but not kill.*

Hey, the times weren't all bad. In fact, they were pretty good. If it hadn't been for the white dragon, I never would have gone to the La Brea Tar Pits with Heather Graham, would never have enjoyed the Vans Warped Tour, would never have held an erection for more than an hour, would never have gotten this book contract. That's something, isn't it? A big long hard boner and a fifty-grand advance? Yes, I know it's over for guys like me, Doris, even if you have a movie deal, which I do. Chuck Norris is a goddamn narc. Stay away from him, and you'll never get caught.

Fuck. Motherfuck. I gotta get off the stuff. I gotta get clean. I gotta call Tom Waits, who understands. I gotta get this high, one more time. Holy shit-faced mother-of-fucking God. I am a fucking junkie.

INTRODUCTION

R ecently, as I entertained a variety of friends and acquaintances (many of whom are employed in publishing and the arts) at my modest yet comfortable summer estate in Malta, it occurred to me that I am almost definitely the greatest writer of my time. I strained to think of others who could challenge my position, but they were too provincial, too tweedy, or too dead. No. I towered above the corroded wreckage that is American letters.

In the course of working on this book, my editor came to agree with me. He wanted to include nothing but my best pieces, but the choosing proved too difficult. We debated, drank heartily, fist-fought over women, and always with a similar culmination. All the pieces were biting, evanescent. Each one forwarded the next, and no matter in what order I presented them, they illuminated the oft-mawkish, pungent carnival that is our life on this planet. "Quite simply," said my editor, as we shared a sampling of that delectable weed, marijuana, "your work represents a comprehensive social, cultural, and political portrait of humanity in the latter half of the twentieth century. It is a Sunday buffet of prose upon which your readers will feast mightily." He forgot to add that it also contains some great sex scenes.

As I reread the bulk of my work in the course of the three weeks it took me to put this collection together, I was reminded of something the Immortal Bard once wrote, in his play about merchants, and about Venice: "Thou art too wild, too rude and bold of voice;

parts that become thee happily enough, and in such eyes as ours appear not faults." How true that is about most books, but not about mine, for the triumphs and tragedies of humanity fall under my jurisdiction, in the humble grab bag of erudition that is me.

By now, my biography is familiar to everyone who has read the advance press. My grandfather was an esteemed senator from Texas. Through the marriages of various relatives, I came to be related to the Kennedys, the Rockefellers, the Hefners, and William Shawn, the former editor of *The New Yorker,* whose stewardship kept that magazine of magazines afloat. At seventeen, after a brilliant Harvard career, I sailed to the South Pacific, where I killed people in the service of Empire. Upon returning, my first novel, *Killing People in the Service of Empire,* won the National Book Award. My three subsequent books, each about a different era of history, were highly experimental. The first was fiction, the next journalism, and the last, poetry. All of them changed literature forever until the next book, which changed literature again. I then wrote my own version of the Bible, which sold well and was adapted into a Tony Award–winning musical called *Neal Pollack Presents the Bible.* In 1978, I began weekly broadcasts of *American Tapestry,* the Peabody Award–winning show that created modern radio.

But perhaps I ramble. Is it really appropriate to refer to this world as *my* world, to the time I have lived as *my* time? Why the hell not, you might ask, and please ask away, my friends. For when I began my career, so many decades ago, as a simple hack with a pen, notebook, and ample trust fund, I had no idea what I would encounter. I had never seen a revolution or an execution, never breathed the salty peninsular air of Patagonia or snorted an electric line of rock off the pulsating ass of a porn star. Now I have experienced all those things, but I still feel, inside, like the little boy FDR once called "era-transforming."

In 1968, speaking simultaneously at the Rand Institute's Conference on Extending the War in Vietnam and the People's Park Mud Bath Fuck-In, I had this to say about myself: "There is no reason to believe that I am not the greatest writer who has ever lived.

The world holds no mystery that I cannot solve, no dilemma that I cannot understand. It is as if I am everywhere and nowhere at once, yet still have time to meet you for lunch. Of course you have questions. Who doesn't? What is the nature of love? Why is there a moon? How do we endure? It is my job to deal with these unholy predicaments, because I can, and because people pay me. If there is one rule in writing, it is this: I am the best."

The pieces contained within this volume have a complex organization. It is neither chronological nor thematic, yet it necessarily contains elements of both chronology and theme. Like other writes who craft postmodern narratives—Cortázar, Calvino, Gaddis, among others—my work operates with an internal logic. This book is a post-Joycean, post-Proustian journey into the one thing that no living writer other than me can explore—the truth about the ultimate destiny of the human soul. For no matter what I have seen in my life, the war, hunger, misery, broken promises, and forgotten love, one thing has remained steadfast. Myself. Throughout my life, I have been there.

Go, then, my noble readers. Explore this book, with your minds, with your hearts, and with your friends. It will stir your blood and shake your bones. If, on my book tour, I have occasion to meet, or even sleep with, you, let my astonishing meditative and narrative powers give you fortitude when I have motored on to the next American hamlet. From the earliest piece collected here, written when I was still an unsophisticated virgin living in Paris, to the last, written approximately five minutes ago, this book is your world, and mine. The interlocking lattice of history and style and the sluice pipe of destiny have merged our private lives with our political selves, all attached by the word of words, that most mysterious word of all. Money. Money!

NP
Wellfleet
Cape Cod, Massachusetts
May 2000

CHRONOLOGY

DATE	AUTHOR'S LIFE	LITERARY CONTEXT	HISTORICAL EVENTS
A.D. 0			Jesus Christ born in Bethlehem.
1930	Neal Pollack born in Boston.	Faulkner: *As I Lay Dying*.	Gandhi begins civil disobedience campaign.
1931	Travels to India with parents.	Faulkner: *Sanctuary*.	Nazi Party consolidates power in Germany.
1936	Begins fourth grade. Publishes essay, "Does Faulkner Write Too Many Novels?" in *American Mercury*.	Faulkner: *Absalom, Absalom* Nabokov: *Despair*.	Spanish Civil War begins.
1938	Goes to Spain as junior correspondent for *New York Herald Tribune*. Befriends George Orwell.	Orwell: *Homage to Catalonia*.	Germany annexes Austria.
1941	Youngest student ever at Exeter.	Fitzgerald: *The Last Tycoon*.	Germany invades USSR.
1942	Mother dies.	Camus: *The Stranger*.	The world at war.
1943	Rooms with Wally Trumbull. Has erotic awakening. Learns meaning of tenderness.	Nothing special.	Germany on the run.
1945	Enters Harvard as junior. Graduates Harvard.	Orwell: *Animal Farm*.	Hitler commits suicide. WWII ends.
1947	Ships out for Philippines with Wally Trumbull, who is stabbed during game of Pai Gow poker.	*The Diary of Anne Frank*.	Indian Independence Act. Truman delivers "No More Pessimistic Literature" speech. World rejoices in eternal peace.
1948	Publishes *The Brutal, Racist Murder of Wally Trumbull*. Wins National Book Award.	Greene: *The Heart of the Matter*.	Gandhi assassinated. Israel created. Apartheid introduced in South Africa.

DATE	AUTHOR'S LIFE	LITERARY CONTEXT	HISTORICAL EVENTS
1950	*From India to Israel to South Africa: One Traveler's Journey.* Moves to Paris. Called "greatest young writer alive" by Hemingway. Has frequent sexual relations.	Salinger: *The Catcher in the Rye.*	Germany is divided.
1953	*Salinger Alone; Europe: The Forgotten Continent.* Marries the novelist Mary McCarthy. Divorces the novelist Mary McCarthy.	Nabokov: *Lolita.*	Josef Stalin dies.
1957	Publishes biography of Stalin. Plots with Nabokov to kill Pasternak. Hangs out with the Beats. Spends time in Cuba with Castro.	Pasternak: *Doctor Zhivago.* Ginsberg: *Howl (or, The Ballad of Pollack).*	America seethes with paranoia.
1959	Goes to Hollywood. Blacklisted.	Achebe: *Things Fall Apart.*	Castro seizes power in Cuba.
1963	*Give Spain a Chance.* Marries the actress Claire Bloom. Wins second National Book Award. Volunteers as subject for Air Force LSD tests. Publishes essay, *"Why South America Can Never Produce a Great Novel,"* in *The Saturday Review.*	N/A	John F. Kennedy assassinated.
1967	Marriage to Claire Bloom annulled. Proclaims Summer of Love "roaring bullshit carnival."	García Márquez: *One Hundred Years of Solitude.*	Arab-Israeli Six-Day War.
1968	Publishes *Leon: A Man of the Streets.* Sent to Vietnam by six different magazines.	Solzhenitsyn: *Cancer Ward.*	Martin Luther King Jr. assassinated. Richard Nixon elected U.S. president. *Laugh-In* debuts.
1969	*Hell Here on Earth, Volume II.* Wins third National Book Award. Declines award in protest of Vietnam. Named lifetime member of the Beatles.	Roth: *Goodbye, Columbus.*	Americans land man on moon.

DATE	AUTHOR'S LIFE	LITERARY CONTEXT	HISTORICAL EVENTS
1974	*The Creeping Madness and Other Tales of Equatorial Life.* Accepts Nixon's apology on Dick Cavett show. Meets Nelson Mandela. Declares him "unimpressive."	Bellow: *Humboldt's Gift.*	Nixon resigns.
1976	Accuses Saul Bellow of bribing Swedish Academy.	Carver: *Will You Please Be Quiet, Please?*	Death of Mao Tse-Tung. Saddam Hussein comes to power in Iraq.
1979	*Beware the East: A Voyage Through Iran, Iraq, and China.* Marries novelist Marianne Wiggins. Birth of son Wilfrid.	Calvino: *If on a winter's night a traveler.*	Margaret Thatcher first female prime minister of U.K.; Iran hostage crisis.
1981	*Listening to Silence.* Has affair with Margaret Thatcher. Becomes British citizen.	Updike: *Rabbit Is Rich.*	Ronald Reagan elected U.S. president.
1982	Wins Booker Prize.	García Márquez: *Chronicle of a Death Foretold.*	Falklands War.
1983	Renounces British citizenship over Falklands War.	Narayan: *A Tiger for Malgudi.*	America enters the Second Dark Ages.
1987	Wins PEN/Faulkner Award for *Memories of Myself.* Publishes *An Island Beyond the Stars.* Introduces Marianne Wiggins to Salman Rushdie. Marriage to Marianne Wiggins ends.	Morrison: *Beloved.*	Terry Waite taken hostage in Beirut. Berlin Wall prepares to crumble.
1992	*Jacked In: One Man's Erotic Adventures in Cyberspace.* Briefly edits *The New Yorker.* Sees wraithlike form of Wally Trumbull hovering over bed. Finally visits Germany.	Ondaatje: *The English Patient.*	Bill Clinton elected U.S. president.

DATE	AUTHOR'S LIFE	LITERARY CONTEXT	HISTORICAL EVENTS
1999	*Democratic Perils.* Marries Janeane Garafalo in secret ceremony. Named "Hot Indie Novelist to Watch" by Salon.com. Becomes anarchist. Begins work on *The Neal Pollack Anthology of American Literature.*	Nothing of note.	The Battle in Seattle.
2000	Publishes *The Neal Pollack Anthology of American Literature.* Embarks on seventeen-country, eighty-five-city book tour. Leaves Janeane Garafalo sobbing in bathtub at luxury suite in Mandalay Bay Hotel, Las Vegas.	Eggers: *A Man Called Dave.*	Presidency stolen by Republicans. Ralph Nader burned at stake by ignorant public.
2001	Publishes *At Home with Osama: One Terrorist's Journey.*	The end of irony.	United States attacked.

FAMILY TREE

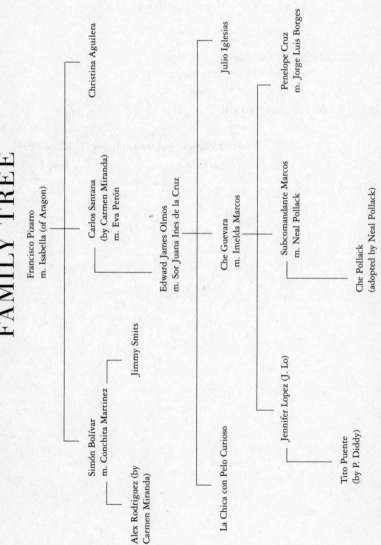

Francisco Pizarro
m. Isabella (of Aragon)

Christina Aguilera

Carlos Santana
(by Carmen Miranda)
m. Eva Perón

Simón Bolívar
m. Conchita Martinez

Jimmy Smits

Alex Rodriguez (by
Carmen Miranda)

Edward James Olmos
m. Sor Juana Ines de la Cruz

Julio Iglesias

Che Guevara
m. Imelda Marcos

Penelope Cruz
m. Jorge Luis Borges

Subcomandante Marcos
m. Neal Pollack

Che Pollack
(adopted by Neal Pollack)

Jennifer Lopez (J. Lo)

La Chica con Pelo Curioso

Tito Puente
(by P. Diddy)

God bless the lot of them, although
I don't remember which was which:
God bless the U.S.A., so large,
So friendly, and so rich.

—Neal Pollack, ghostwriting for W. H. Auden,
June 1963

THE
NEAL POLLACK
ANTHOLOGY
OF AMERICAN
LITERATURE

THE ALBANIA OF
MY EXISTENCE

I've been going to bed lately on a pile of jagged stones covered only by a thin cotton blanket half-eaten by moths. This is one of the worst possible sleeping arrangements I could imagine. Sometimes I wonder how things got this way, but I have to remember that I am a journalist, novelist, radio producer, and poet, and I am here in Albania to find out what life is really like for a family in the poorest country in Europe. I have personally borne witness to much human suffering. People here are beset by unwanted refugees, obscure diseases, and limited opportunities to express themselves through fashion. I must tell you: Things are not good.

We had dirt for lunch today. All twenty-three of us. Jumanji, the patriarch of this family, is a short, bald, armless man who looks older than his eighty-seven years. He tells me that dirt has been of short supply in Albania lately, and he worries about his family's diet. I have tried to make our food taste better using some of the skills that I learned at the Culinary Institute of America, but with no success. My considerable abilities seem useless here; I am a Rhodes scholar, but no one in Albania has even heard of Cambridge, much less of England.

Although this family's house has no plumbing, consistent heat source, or exterior walls, they do have satellite television. I was tired today from all my reporting, so I relaxed by watching CNN's Eastern European Entertainment Minute. I saw that a good friend of mine had won a jury prize at the Sundance Film Festival, which made me think about the awards and honors I've gained in my life, the trophies, the ribbons, and the cash. In the face of this Albanian poverty and hopelessness, they all seem somehow trivial now. Do you know what I mean?

I WAKE UP EARLY this morning and watch the village children play soccer with the bloated carcass of a cat. I've been here so long that this kind of thing doesn't bother me anymore, so I join in. I score three goals and make a game-winning save. The children gather around me and ask about my life in the more bohemian sections of Brooklyn. I show them a picture of my girlfriend.

"She is very beautiful," says one of them.

"Yes," I say, "and very wealthy. She is a human-rights activist who has also written three prize-winning novels."

Later, a man is impaled on a stake in the town square, while a desperate, ravaging mob tears at his clothes to wear as their own. I want to ask: For what crime was this man sentenced to die? But I do not speak Albanian.

I am leaving tomorrow. The town has pooled its remaining money together, three dollars, to throw me a farewell party. I hug Grandma Ninotchka, my favorite family member, for a long time. She works twenty hours a day, six days a week as a pluto- nium miner to feed her family, and spends her precious free time, what little there is, as a volunteer gravedigger.

"You have brought a beacon of hope into our dark and miser- able world," she says. "And God bless you for not stealing my oatmeal like the man from the *New York Times*."

I am not prepared for the immense wave of emotion that I am experiencing. Nothing I went through in college, not even hav- ing dinner with two presidents, could have possible prepared me for this. I cry silent tears, and pray for the people of this sorrow- ridden country, and for myself.

(From *Red Curtain, Blue People,* 1985)

DATELINE: COLOMBIA

I am in Bogotá, alone in my hotel room, listening to the bombs. It is noon, but it might as well be midnight. The light shines diffusely through the cheesecloth curtains that are my only shield from reality. I look out onto the Street of Groans. People in fatigues fling other people in different colored fatigues against a concrete wall, and then the people who have been flung turn on the flingers, and fling them back, cackling with vehement glee. The whole affair is strange to me, but also familiar. I am reminded of Vietnam in 1957, or Madrid in 1934. Sometimes, I am reminded of Omaha in 1973, though I don't know why. I can hear helicopters, and men are marching, and the whiff of tragedy permeates my nostrils.

The man from room service brings me another plate of squid arepas, and I tip him generously.

"There's a drug war going on out there," I say.

"I know, señor," he says, shaking his head with ineluctable sadness, "I know. I pray that, through your work, the American people will listen. That they will learn."

I have not left my hotel room in three weeks, not even to go to the toilet down the hall, which is incessantly flushing, flushing. Fear permeates the air here like rotten meat, and I am afraid. But I know now that the people of Colombia need me, and I will not deny them their freedom.

I call the American embassy and say:

"Prepare my transport. I'm going in country."

* * *

IT IS DAWN in Palanga, a village deep in the Colombian interior, but also near the coast. I sit under a palm, eyes cocked for gunfire, as a female guerrilla in camouflage pants and a Lilith Fair T-shirt stands in the town's concrete center square, squirting mustard onto her heaving breasts.

"I am not supposed to do this with journalists around," she says, "but I recognized your picture from the Great American Writers 2001 Desk Calendar, and I could not resist."

This is a common reaction, I tell her. She asks me what the mustard is like in America, but I don't answer, as I am pondering the failures of our Congress, our captains of industry, our editors of teetering online magazines, to answer the call as we sleepwalk forward into a drug-war abyss from which we will not be able to extricate ourselves, not even with a very long rope. In my notebook, there are questions about war that need to be answered.

"Would you like to meet the leader of my guerrilla group?" asks the woman.

Drawn together by grief in a time of trouble, she and I take a boat ride into the jungle, toward her people, and we make love passionately, intelligently. I ponder my good fortune and journalistic talent.

"The earth moved," she says.

"It always does," say I.

We make love again, in the loam, and I am good.

THERE ARE APPROXIMATELY thirty-five competing rebel groups in Colombia. Many of them have the letters "f" and "a" in their acronyms. They fund themselves through a variety of means, including drug smuggling, kidnapping, bake sales, and sponsoring independent film festivals. Other than that, I know nothing about them, even though my Spanish translations of my own work have won many awards. But the rebels are in revolt against their government, and that's good enough for me.

I have arrived in a clearing in a forest by a river near a mountain where twenty-five young, good-looking people are taking rumba lessons. This is the base camp of the FBAP, a rebel group that my escort assures me is "about to be signed to a major label." The leader of the group, who calls himself El Pistolero (The Pistolero), is in his tent, playing chess on his computer. He has a DSL line, he tells me, and he regularly participates in outer-space-themed role-playing games with students from Oberlin College in Ohio.

"Hey, man," I say, "you got any coke?"

Later, the clouds are yellow and the sky is blue, and the rim of the horizon runs across the lip of the landscape, a band of hope in a world of pain. The rebels and I snort fat lines of the purest shit ever. We shoot our machine guns into the air, and the peasants scatter. Many things are set on fire, and in the loamy dusk, we watch the jungle burn. I shake my head, with joy, with grief, and because it is so damn itchy.

Night falls, as it must, and I get to thinking that it is time to provide a solution to our war on drugs. I have confidence that it will come to me, perhaps in the form of a screenplay set partly in Mexico. I also think it would be interesting to make a movie about a drug czar's teenage daughter who becomes a junkie whore because she feels alienated from her suburban surroundings. That would be so realistic, and the pain would make America weep.

They tell me that another reporter is arriving today, but I know, somehow, that his interviewing technique won't be as interesting as mine. I stand atop a hill, looking down. Time moves forward and backward, and I vomit on my shoes. These are the last days of Colombia in its current incarnation.

Thank God I was here.

(From *The Hunger of Bogotá,* 1986)

I AM FRIENDS WITH
A WORKING-CLASS
BLACK WOMAN

I'm sitting at the kitchen table in a low-rise South Bronx apartment building, waiting for my subject, Cora Johnson, to come home from work. All day, I've been exhaustively cataloging everything in Cora's apartment, taking notes, and talking into a microcassette recorder. As a magazine reporter, which is my profession, I want to find out everything I can about Cora's world, about the life of a working-class black woman.

The day hasn't exactly been lonely. Cora's mother, who is also named Cora, has joined me; the family calls her Old Cora, even though she is only forty-five. Also in the apartment are Cora's four-year-old son Lattrellquon, and seventeen babies from the neighborhood, all under the age of two, that Old Cora cares for every day, free of charge.

"It used to be different around here," Old Cora tells me. "For instance, the stove used to work."

I wonder what it would be like to not have a working stove. In fact, I feel so lucky, so very lucky to have not one, but two in my own house. My fiancée and I love to have friends over for dinner and try out new recipes that we've picked up on our travels.

"It must be hard not to have a stove," I say to Old Cora.

"Yeah." She chuckles. "It makes it awful hard to cook."

My subject, Young Cora, comes home from her downtown data-processing job. Our time together has been limited so far. At night, to earn extra money, she works as a security guard at an aluminum-processing plant on Long Island. Four mornings a week, she wakes up at five for a third job, as an apprentice dog groomer. On the weekends, she toils at a Colombian bakery in Queens. In all, Cora tells me, she gets about ten hours of sleep a week.

I think about the differences between Young Cora and myself. She is thirty-one years old, and already a grandmother of three. Here I am, and I have no children, though I do have twenty-five godchildren in six different countries. She has four bad-paying jobs that don't offer her health insurance or day care. I have no fixed job at all, really, but plenty of money and lots of famous, successful, attractive friends. She didn't finish high school. I didn't finish my second Ph.D. thesis, but I realize it's not the same. Somehow, the divide between us doesn't seem fair.

Early one morning last summer, I rented a car and picked Cora up so I could take her to work. We were both obviously tired, so we didn't talk much. As I drove in silence, a morning-show host made tasteless jokes about our former president's sex life. Cora chuckled.

"Boy, that Clinton, he sure does get himself in some messes," she said.

"Yeah," I replied. "He sure does."

We looked at each other, and burst out laughing, big, gut-wrenching belly laughs, tear-inducing howls of mirth. Then I realized: I was friends with this woman, this Cora Johnson, this subject of mine. I'd had black friends before. My favorite play-mate as a child was the son of the ambassador from Ghana, and I was on more-than-acquaintance terms with Savion Glover, Henry Louis Gates Jr., and Anna Deveare Smith. Indeed, Carmela, my Brazilian fiancée, is one-quarter black herself. But Cora was my first working-class black friend, and I felt so proud.

Working-class black women are not a new phenomenon in the Bronx. Cora Johnson's family has been mostly working class ever since they migrated from the small southern hamlet of Weasel, Alabama, in 1948, after Old Cora's father, Henry, got a fifteen-dollar-an-hour union job as a taster at a New Jersey petrochemical plant. The Bronx's population of working-class black women grew from seven in 1930 to thirty-six in 1940 to 15,453 in 1950. It currently stands at 78,765, and appears to be stabilizing. At the same time, real wages in America have declined, which is a shame.

As my research moved ahead and I spent more time with Cora and her family, I realized the stark differences between our two cultures. One evening at Cora's apartment, we sat around the television and watched *Malcolm & Eddie,* a sitcom starring Malcolm-Jamal Warner, who I vaguely remembered as the teenage son from *The Cosby Show.* In the room were Cora, Old Cora, Cora's uncle, an aging black nationalist named Hampton Muhammad, and myself. We were also joined from time to time by Cora's son Lattrellquon, her sisters Doris and LaSheena, Doris's three kids, several neighbor women whose names I never learned, and LaSheena's boyfriend, a mysterious, hulking figure with an eye patch and a Van Dyke beard who referred to himself only as "The Archangel."

The program was repulsive and stupid, and I refused to cloak my displeasure. I snorted, grunted, and snarled. The entire half hour, I don't think I laughed once. Even more disturbing was the fact that Cora's family seemed to enjoy themselves immensely. They especially liked the show's climax, where Eddie gets trapped in a washing machine while spying on the locker room of a women's basketball team.

After the show ended, I made a comment that I was offended by some of Malcolm and Eddie's homophobic asides to each other. Cora's family didn't seem interested. They just wanted to watch the next show. I remembered a passage I had read in a social-science journal that I'd started subscribing to in preparation for this article. "Just like white people," it said, "black people also enjoy watching television uncritically, even mindlessly."

But I wasn't satisfied. These people were comfortable laughing at Malcolm and Eddie, and I wasn't. I felt the accumulated hatred of hundreds of years in their searing stares as I stammered through an explanation of why I thought homophobia was wrong. Ossified decades-old bitterness hung over Cora's living room like a living, breathing, flying animal, waiting for a snack. I couldn't stand it any longer.

"Please understand me!" I shouted, desperately. "I don't want your hatred! It's not my fault that I went to Exeter and Harvard! I can't help the fact that I founded an avant-garde theater company in the East Village! My appearances on MSNBC mean nothing to me! I have traveled over most of the world, and have seen so many things, so much poverty, and so much war! I have written extensively about people in trouble! Don't you see? I am not a representative of everything you hate! I'm myself. Not a working-class black woman or an upper-middle-class white journalist and author who's engaged to a beautiful Brazilian law professor! Just myself! And I don't think Malcolm and Eddie are funny!"

They stared at me blankly. The Archangel reached into his coat, and for a moment I thought he was going to pull a gun and plug me right there. I flung myself behind the sofa. He took a lighter out of his pocket and lit a cigarette.

The family howled.

"I thought you were going to shoot me," I said.

"Naw," said the Archangel. "One more arrest and I'm in jail for life."

Uncle Hampton Muhammad said, "You white people always think we're going to shoot you."

"Not always . . ." I said.

"Yes," he said sadly. "Always."

I began to cry, out of both fear and grief. Cora moved behind the sofa and pulled me into her strong, tired, working-class arms. She said her family forgave me, that they loved me, that they accepted me as one of them. At last, the divide was closed.

Together we had closed the divide.

Cora and I talked well into the night, sometimes on the record, sometimes off, sometimes sobbing, sometimes dry-eyed. Our relationship wasn't going to end any time soon. We had so much work yet left to do.

"I have never felt more proud to be a journalist," I told her. "Never."

Cora took my hand tenderly, and told me she was also proud, proud to be my friend. I felt good and warm inside. I smiled at my friend Cora, my friend, the working-class black woman.

(From *Leon: Return to the Streets,* 1996)

IT IS EASY TO TAKE A
LOVER IN CUBA

From where I sit, thirty-five thousand feet in the air, Cuba glistens in the distance, like a glistening jewel. But I cannot truly see it, not like I should. I open my wallet and pull out a picture of my girlfriend. Giselle. She is half-Portuguese, half-French. She holds a Ph.D. in international relations from Princeton, and is a featured dancer in the Joffrey Ballet. Often when we walk down the street in Brooklyn, strangers of all races and genders say to me, "You have the most beautiful girlfriend I have ever seen," and they are correct.

It's only been five hours since I last held Giselle, but already I am full of longing. "Giselle!" I sigh to myself. "How I wish you could come to Cuba with me!"

My seatmate is a phlegmatic middle-aged German named Heinrich. He asks me why I'm making this trip. I tell him that I've received an assignment from a prominent American magazine to write about what it's like to visit Cuba on assignment from a prominent American magazine.

"What about you?" I ask.

"I have ten reasons," he says, "and they're all named Pussy."

Have I heard him correctly? Is he really coming to Cuba for sex? I'm shocked, and I tell him so.

"You do not understand," he says, pointing to my picture of

Giselle. "That woman, in Cuba, is just average. You can have sex any time of the day, with anyone you want, for almost no money at all. Cuba is a paradise of lovemaking. It is the holy land of sexual freedom."

"Well, I have no interest. I am with my girlfriend, monogamously."

"You say that now," Heinrich nearly whispers as we begin our final descent, "but your opinion will change. It is easy to take a lover in Cuba. You will see. You will see . . ."

My heart whimpers. My feet sweat. I am overcome by a thrill not unlike religious ecstasy. Cuba! Lost marvel of the Caribbean! What sweetness, what magic, what treasures do you contain within your swelling, magnificent hills?

I AM EXHAUSTED as I drag my luggage through security. My God. The customs officer is splendid. Her lips are like soft, pale-red balloons, her skin like beautiful tea. Her eyes, the color of the clearest blue lake, shoot laser beams of desire at my heart. From her name tag, I can see that she is named Carmela.

"Come with me," she says. "You have a security problem."

She takes me into a small office and draws the shade.

"I only cost two dollars," she says.

She is offering me sex. I am not prepared for this. Why, I haven't even yet left the airport!

"I have a girlfriend," I say in perfect Spanish, "and I love her."

Carmela whips back her head and laughs. Her long hair is like black wheat waving in a cool wind.

"Oh you American!" she says. "Would you have me eat leftover dung for dinner?"

She removes her uniform top; her breasts are like milk, or cream. No. More like eggs, or perhaps a combination of the three. They are a kind of breast custard.

"I can't . . ." I say, weakly, but I no longer mean it. Five minutes in Cuba, and already its wondrous charms have overwhelmed.

* * *

THE MOON REFLECTS crude shadows off the hood of the Jeep that I've rented for thirty-five cents a week. My companions are a Russian gun smuggler named Vlad, a young British lawyer named Malcolm, and Lars, a professional clown from Sweden. We drive through the pitted streets of Havana Vieja, with one destination in mind: La Casa de Doña Angelica, Havana's most famous, and cheapest, brothel.

I have been in Cuba for eight days now, and have had sex with sixty-five different women. Some of them I have paid up to ten dollars, but most have asked for less. One woman rode me silly for several hours in exchange for a pair of sneakers. Another fellated me for a bag of pretzels. Still another became my slave for a day after I gave her my copy of *The New Yorker*'s summer fiction issue.

"Why do you all do this so willingly?" I asked one, as we lay naked while her ceiling fan played dusty tricks on the peeling wall.

"Don't you know?" she said. "All our lives, we Cuban women have dreamed of making love with an American man! That is why I care for you so, more than all the others. You are so handsome, so accomplished! Tell me again about your appearances on CNBC!"

I talked to her a while, softly, about the media. Suddenly, she began to weep.

"Can I have a dollar?" she asked. "Please! My children are so hungry!"

These Cubanas know how to ask for money, and when. But they always tell me that I'm different, better, than the men who seek solely to exploit them, and I'm glad they realize the difference.

I stop the Jeep in front of the whorehouse. The other men leap out eagerly, without reflection. I stare at the moon briefly and think of Giselle. But right now, she seems very, very far away.

THE TINY TOWN of Santa Puta de la Chingada, on the eastern coast, is markedly different from Havana. There are more trees, fewer cars. People seem to eat more fish here.

I have heard of an elderly woman named Esmerelda who rents a small cabana on the coast. When I approach her house, she's cleaning her teeth with the sharpened hoof of a goat. Immediately, I feel that she's someone with whom I can talk.

"My time here has disturbed me greatly," I say one night, as we flick fish bones into the water. "I know I've cheated on my girlfriend, but I couldn't help myself. It was so easy. The women simply desired me too much."

Esmerelda breaks an egg on her forehead. The onrushing surf sounds like waves beating against the shore as I wait for her to speak.

"Ay, *jovencito*," she says. "You do not understand. These women will do anything to get to Havana, even steal a scooter from a small child. The city is where the foreign men are, and the foreign men, despite their repulsive smells, have the money."

"But the things they said to me!" I exclaim.

"We give classes," says the woman. "Those of us who remember life before the revolution know how to massage the American ego. We know what a writer wants to hear. We were all acquainted with Hemingway. Now there was a man! Nothing like these weak magazine types with their pathetic per diems."

Esmerelda extinguishes a cigar on the back of her hand and spits into a cup bearing the likeness of Pluto, Mickey Mouse's dog. I begin to sob uncontrollably. Without intention, I have realized an essential aspect of my nature.

"Why are we all so cruel to one another?" I shout into the howling, bitter wind.

"That is the nature of man, *mi hijo*," says the woman sadly. "The only solace we can take is in the arms of a lover."

She is, of course, correct. I have never needed the soothing touch of woman more than I do right now.

Giselle! Oh God! My Giselle!

"But there are no women here!" I say.

"What am I," says Esmerelda. *"Un camaron?"*

I look at her head, which is topped with just a few stray wisps of long, gray hair. She has no teeth. Her arms are shrunken and withered, like shrunken, withered arms. Her feet are gnarled and almost entirely without toenails. This woman is old, very old. But I feel that it would be rude to compare her with a shrimp.

"Of course not," I say. "You are a woman. A beautiful woman."

"If you really think so," she says, "for three dollars I can heal you. I may be a shriveled witch hag, but I am still capable of giving pleasure."

Even before she reaches the end of her sentence, I realize that I will satisfy my longing, my lust, with this woman, for she is a mirror of Cuban essence, a living, golden vein of Cuban memory. At that precise moment, I capitulate, and as I do so, suddenly everything I have ever written is unrepeatable since time immemorial and forever more, because freelance journalists who have sex with a one-hundred-year-old woman do not have a second opportunity on earth.

(From *An Island Beyond the Stars,* 1987)

MEMORIES OF
TIMES SQUARE

Before Mayor Giuliani went on his rampage against sex shops in New York, brutally reducing their number from 144 to 142, Times Square was a paradise of sleaze, a carnival of smut, a festival of naughty, naughty boys and girls. It was the greatest place in the world to spend a weekend if you were drunk, and if you weren't, it was the greatest place in the world to get drunk and spend a weekend. How do I know all this, you might ask? Well, I will tell you.

I spent most of the 1970s as a tabloid reporter, and my beat was midtown Manhattan. I have memories, fond, dark memories of smack and rain-drenched alleys and a never-ending beat box called freedom. Those were the times when the times were good, when you could buy the *New York Times* for a quarter and spend your time having the time of your life and still be home in time for dinner. Those were some glorious times, the times I spent in Times Square. I share them with you now in the spirit of sharing. Let me don that fur coat I used to wear without fear of political reprisal. Let's you and me get it on, Times Square style.

AT THE CORNER of Forty-second and Fifth Avenue, there was a dwarf. We called him Stewart the Dwarf, because that's what he was. Stewart juggled sex toys. Dildos were his specialty. He could hoist a dozen dildos into the air at once, and keep them up there, all the while spraying the crowd with an array of snappy patter. It went something like this: "Hey yo dildos, juggling dildos, up in the air, dildos dildos." My newsroom buddies and I could watch Stewart for hours. At around 6 P.M., he would break out the fruit-flavored creams, ooze them onto his arms, and begin juggling whips, which he intermittently cracked at passersby. He had a makeshift leather sling that he hung between newspaper boxes, and he'd swing there, making balloon animals out of condoms, handing them to frightened children. Occasionally, the police would arrest him on some trumped-up vice charge, but the next day, Stewart would be on the sidewalk again, juggling. "Billy Barty bailed me out," he'd say, and we'd laugh and laugh.

I KNEW A prostitute who went by the name Tristan Isolde. She was a real dish, and a lady to boot. One summer, she cut a deal with the guy who ran TKTS and he let her work the booth on alternate Thursdays. For thirty-five dollars, she offered a mezzanine seat for *Annie* and two hours at the Chelsea Hotel. Fifty clams got you a balcony seat for *The Tap Dance Kid* and a three-way at Port Authority. For one hundred dollars, she would perform the entire soundtrack of *Dreamgirls* in a bathtub, complete with Nell Carter mask. I was partial to her Mummenschanz special, for obvious reasons. One night a couple of years ago, I ran into her at a roast-pork joint on the Lower East Side. She'd been working as a legal secretary, she told me, and was married now, with a kid. "It wasn't the same after *Miss Saigon*," she said. "Suddenly, being a prostitute wasn't cool anymore." I sighed and gazed into my rice and beans, thinking, Andrew Lloyd Webber ruined everything.

THE NEON ASS, a gay nightclub on Forty-third Street, had its special charms. With your ten-dollar admission fee, you received a gram of fine-grade Peruvian cocaine, a gigolo, a basket of joints, and a choice of flavored PCPs. From there, you can only guess what happened, but I can tell you that it was pretty hot. Your actions had no consequences, and it felt like the song would go on forever.

* * *

SOMETIMES, IF IT was late at night and I was hopped up on green-ies, I'd run into a pimp I knew named Lucky Wilbur. In clothing and bone structure, he greatly resembled Antonio Fargas from *Starsky and Hutch,* only his behavior was far less stereotypical. This may have been because Wilbur traded only in household pets, and not for sexual purposes. "Just around the corner, there's a real fine basset hound for you," he said the first time we met. "Name of Lyman. A hundred bucks for the weekend, and he won't pee on your slippers." I would usually say no to Wilbur, but occasionally I would wake on a gin-soaked morning and find a cocker curled next to me, or a Persian scratching the leg of my dresser. "I got some of the nicest pussies in town," Wilbur would say. "You can pet them and pet them and they will never get tired and always be your friend, and they love to play with your balls." He didn't have much of an ear for euphemism, no matter how obvious.

WHEN I WALK past the Disney stores and the theme restaurants and all the happy families these days, I have to sigh, mostly because I now have a severe respiratory disorder. The memories come flooding back to me, like floods do when you remember them, and I recall all the strippers, whores, junkies, and perverts I knew back in the day. Some of them are in the pen now, others in the suburbs. One, who shall remain nameless, is a congressman from Virginia. But mostly, they are ghosts.

The other day, I swear I saw a dwarf out of the corner of my mind's eye. I turned and shouted "Stewart!" half expecting a dildo to fly past my head. But it was only a very short man. He was from Nebraska, and he was taking a photo of a statue of Matt Lauer. I felt very sad. The man walked away into the freshly scrubbed Times Square afternoon, and, after a coughing fit that lasted several minutes and nearly killed me, so, reluctantly, did I.

(From *Satan's Pocket: The Death of An American Neighborhood,* 1999)

PORTRAIT OF
AN ANDALUSIAN
HORSE TRAINER

At 3:30 A.M. on a recent Tuesday, Paolo Luciamonte, the last great Andalusian horse trainer, leapt from his bed like a man thirty years younger, spat on the hard, cold floor like a man thirty years older, and put a fresh pot of coffee on the stove like a man almost exactly his age. As the sweet fog of untroubled sleep evaporated from Paolo's brain, he stared out his kitchen window into the crisp high-mountain dawn, like he'd done every morning since the day after he was born.

The colt loomed monstrously in front of a swirling wall of rain clouds. He was El Caballo de Sangre, the Horse of Blood. The death horse. He was the greatest challenge Paolo Luciamonte had ever faced.

"Today is the day I will break the spirit of the Horse of Blood," Paolo muttered into his cup of steaming brew. "Today he will learn. No horse is useful unless he can be ridden for money. No horse is free in my stable."

I had come to Andalusia as a reporter to discover what it was like for a man who had never known any other way of life to train horses in a world that had increasingly less use for his services. As I'd driven the previous night down the highway from the

23

Barcelona airport toward Rancho Luciamonte, listening to a Macy Gray CD on my Discman, I thought about my grandfather, who had trained horses himself at our family ranch in Texas while I was growing up. It was a harder yet easier time, simultaneously wealthier and more poverty-stricken, softly innocent, yet also very guilty.

I marveled at what a different person I'd turned out to be than my grandfather, he the world's largest manufacturer of tube socks and low-grade nuclear weapons, me a freelance magazine writer, published novelist, founder of an experimental kindergarten in the Bronx, and male fashion model. Long ago, it seemed that I was on a different track, one that was far less compelling than the world of fame and accomplishment in which I now reside.

In the summers of my puissant youth, when I wasn't on the island of Corfu with my parents and Jackie Onassis and Andy Warhol, I was in Texas, riding horses with my grandfather. When we weren't riding them, we were breeding them. When we weren't breeding them, we were racing them. Sometimes, we were even feeding them. Horses spurred us to great passions, and I pranced mine relentlessly, until that day Grandpa made me take a special ride.

My grandfather retained the services of a Nubian manservant named Carlos, who was exceedingly large, nearly twice my adult size, and I've been told by everyone with whom I've had sex, a lot of women, believe me, that I have a nice body. The night I changed forever, Grandpa and I were counting my inheritance money in front of a roaring fire. He called Carlos into the room.

"Carlos," he said, "it's time to play horsey."

Although Carlos protested, Grandpa soon had him whinnying, balanced on his massive forearms and ample knees. He then placed me astride his houseboy's firm, hulking back, thrust a whip into my hand, and said:

"Don't just sit there boy, make Carlos giddyap!"

"But . . ." I protested.

"Don't worry," said Grandpa. "Carlos likes being a horsey, don't you, Carlos?"

Carlos, who had a stainless-steel bit jammed between his teeth, could not respond. Grandpa thrust a cruel, pointy boot into Carlos's resilient, meaty hindquarters, and Carlos began to move. As I trotted him around the room, I asked Grandpa why he was making me do this hideous, slave-driving thing.

"Boy," Grandpa said, "there are two kinds of men in life: Trainers and horses! And for us, every other man is a horse, black or white! Remember that! Don't ever let another man saddle you up and get you into a lather!"

Instinctively, I sensed that Grandpa was a little off on this one.

"Whoa, Carlos!" I shouted. "Whoa!"

I dismounted the debased Nubian and turned to my grandfather.

"I don't want your stinking golden bridle!" I shouted. "I'm gonna make my own way in the world!"

I ran out of the ranch, down the ten-mile-long driveway, and onto the county road. I sobbed and cursed the day I was born. I was seventeen years old and already a Harvard graduate, but what did that mean when I had a super-rich racist grandpa?

Now here I was, in Andalusia, watching Paolo Luciamonte, the last of the great Andalusian horse trainers, get tossed around like Raggedy Andy by El Caballo de Sangre, the Horse of Blood.

"This was to be my day of greatest triumph," he said to me. "But instead, I have just ruined another pair of blue jeans. I cannot defeat this horse. This is the last great horse in the world. No man can tame El Caballo de Sangre, the Horse of Blood. It cannot be done."

The Horse of Blood snorted in equine defiance. Paolo sighed and shook his meaty, weathered fist at the hell stallion.

"I will grind you into mere sausage," he said. "Someday. Someday."

Suddenly, a feeling seized me that was equal parts nostalgia, anger, and book idea.

"Paolo," I said. "May I try riding El Caballo de Sangre? The Horse of Blood?"

"Great Journalist from Brooklyn, you will surely be killed!" Paolo said in heavily accented English. "I, the greatest horse trainer in Andalusia, mount him every day, and he's turned my nuts into butter! What chance do you stand?"

"Let me attempt this feat," I said. "It's for the good of my story, which I am writing for an important magazine with a large circulation."

Paolo sighed angrily, and turned away. He could not bear to witness my bitter ride, and also could not understand that this was a decision into which I had been thrust by destiny. I had come to Andalusia to write a story, but my mission had suddenly been obscured by the darkness of memory. The tragic last years of a centuries-old way of life are nothing compared to my wine-dark soul's screaming need for redemption.

Paolo loped back to the house, where he prepared an omelet made from the eggs of the soon-to-be-extinct Andalusian blue condor. He watched from the house as the sun began its inevitable descent below the great horizon of the grassy plain. I mounted El Caballo de Sangre, the Horse of Blood, and dug man-made stirrups into his flesh with my powerful spurs.

"This one's for you, Carlos," I grunted, and I rode the son of a bitch into the dirt.

(From *Give Spain a Chance,* 1953)

THE BURDEN OF
INTERNET CELEBRITY

As I hunch anew before the ominous Gorgon that is my computer, the cathode glow from the screen seems to me the waning light of the apocalypse itself. Will I be able to endure twenty-four more hours of rampaging notoriety? Will the gods endow me with the will to satisfy my ample fan base? I cannot assume how much E-mail I will receive, because when I guess, I am always wrong. Two thousand? Three thousand? Thirty-two thousand? Will my Web page suffer a million hits, even though it is nearly Christmas? How many screen-freezes will I cause? How many browsers can one man, naked and bleary, possibly engage?

It is not yet 5 A.M., and already the first jolt of caffeine begins the leg-twitching odyssey that is my day. Between my life on the Web and my triathlon training, I will barely have enough time to travel with George Clinton to Brazil, so I can finish a documentary film that my best friend has asked me to narrate. I want to get some writing in before the reporters start calling. Yesterday, it was *Newsweek,* the day before the *Journal.* They all ask the same question, sometimes formulated cleverly, sometimes not. How does it feel, they ask, to be an Internet celebrity?

I chirp and coo and wax technologic, tell them that my life goes on much as before. But these are untruths. I've heard that life is hard, but have discovered that a famous life is nearly unbearably so. My life is not private any longer, but neither is it really public. Rather, it's a kind of quasi-private-pseudo-public life that could only exist in the netherworld of the Internet. I have given myself up to the Web, and like a beast in a cage that eats meat all the time, the Web constantly, insatiably, demands more.

My problems began two years ago, when a good friend of mine from college (who, in the spirit of full disclosure, happens to be the founder of an online magazine for which I write a column and we also have oral sex, once in a while) suggested that I develop a Web page for myself. At the time, I had no idea how to go about designing for the Web, but like everything else in my life, I easily learned the skills in a few hours. Almost immediately, my site, on which I included everything I'd ever written as well as suggestive pictures, was getting thousands of hits per day. I was the subject of feature articles, and became a much-sought-after radio interview subject.

Because I was feeling mischievous, radical, even, I decided to set up a camera in my bedroom to take a picture of me every five minutes, which increased my popularity even further. After that, I wired myself for sound, put another camera in the bathroom, and soon I was being deluged by fan mail from all over the world.

At first, I found the attention enthralling. After all, it had been several years since my first film had won the jury prize at Toronto, and I missed the adulation. Many of the E-mails I received were from young women who wanted to have sex with me. I declined their offers, but agreed to meet a few of them in a chat room for online "orgies."

A sophomore from Iowa State University wrote me, begging me to father her child. I denied her request. Still, she replied a few weeks later.

"I've had myself artificially inseminated at a local clinic," she said, "and I'm naming the baby after you."

The camera takes another picture. My head is cocked jauntily to the left, my "Nirvana Road Crew—1989" T-shirt, given to me by Kurt himself after the tour, features prominently in the view. The pale-blue light of the World Wide Web illuminates the very chin dimple that Winona Ryder once called "extraordinary." Meanwhile, the microphone picks up every groan, shuffle, and phone call from Dan Rather's producer. Does the world really need to know that I'm writing an article for *Vanity Fair*? Who really cares that I'm now a featured essayist on *All Things Considered*? Why does it matter to anyone that I'm on the Grammy selection committee?

There is a reason.

Recently, I was in Rwanda, working on a dispatch for a major European newsmagazine. Our guide took us to a local church, where Hutus had murdered Tutsis, or Tutsis Hutus, and left the bones to blanch. Curious, bald, flea-bitten children dressed in raggy military fatigues gathered around us, staring, pointing, and gaping.

A peanut of a boy, no older than eight, tugged at my pants leg. I was prepared to give him some of my emergency supply of Tootsie Pops.

"Excuse me?" he said. "Sir?"

"Yes, son," I said. "I have candy."

"I don't want candy," said the boy. "I just wanted to say hello."

"Oh," I said. "Hello."

"My friends and I enjoy your Web page very much," he said. "It is often the only ray of hope in the waking tragedy that is our life."

A silent sob moved up from my stomach into my throat. I had to cover my mouth to hold back my cries.

"Oh, God," I said. "Thank you so much."

"We especially like the times when the camera catches you masturbating," said the boy. "It is like a guide from heaven."

I suddenly realized why I had gone onto the Internet. It wasn't to amuse millions of bored college students and television-news-program interns. It wasn't to titillate housewives at lunch-time. It wasn't to sell copies of my most recent book of short stories, now available in paperback from Vintage. No.

For very ten thousand fraternity boys and sorority sisters who were seeking a cheap thrill from my page, at least one Third World prepubescent sought legitimate instruction. This Rwan-dan boy and his friends were being taught a lesson in creative autoeroticism. By me. Over the Internet. From my bedroom in the surprisingly hip Brooklyn neighborhood in which I live, for a few brief minutes every day somewhere in the world, my little Web page was helping to ease the pain of genocide.

"Thank you again, sir," said the boy.

"No," I said, "thank you."

I handed him my entire store of Tootsie Pops. The boy's eyes opened wider than the broiling midday East African sun.

"Now get out of here, kid," I said. "Go home and touch your-self."

As the boy ran away gleaming, I knew that I would never doubt the Internet again.

(From *Jacked In: One Man's Erotic Adventures in Cyberspace,* 1995)

INTERLUDE:
THE OPRAH WINFREY SHOW
March 15, 1996

In my career, I have appeared on many television programs. I developed dear relationships with a variety of hosts, including Steve Allen, Dick Cavett, Arsenio Hall, Charlie Rose, and, most recently, the divine Oprah Winfrey. Twice, she has selected my novels for her Book Club. *Leon: A Man of the Streets* was so honored nearly thirty years after its publication, and recently, Oprah helped launch *Fragments Without Forgetting* into the seemingly impenetrable national consciousness. Oprah has expanded my readership like no television program ever; not even my brief stint on *Laugh-In* gave me such wide exposure to Ma and Pa United States. In her opening editorial for the third issue of *O Magazine,* of which I received an advance copy, Oprah said this about my work: "Neal inspires me like no other writer ever has. His deep understanding of family dynamics and the nature of love transcends race, leaps over gender, and bamboozles sexual orientation. For tenderness mixed with sad truth, no one tops Neal Pollack. Not in my Book Club, anyway."

On March 15, 1996, I watched backstage as Oprah interviewed her other favorite author, Toni Morrison, about *Song of Solomon,* which was that month's club selection. Soon I was to appear on television once again, this time as a surprise guest. It was, quite simply, my pleasure. A partial transcript follows.

OPRAH WINFREY: Toni, in this wonderful book, you create such vivid characters. The scenes are so real. They speak the *truth* about black people in America. How do you come up with them?

TONI MORRISON: Well, I have a spectacular imagination. Obviously, I've never known anyone named Milkman Dead.

OW: I would hope not. [Laughter.] But still, you must draw *some* inspiration from real life.

TM: I do, of course. No writer can exist in a vacuum. But I also read a lot.

OW: What writers have influenced you the most?

TM: Well, Zora Neale Hurston, of course, and Langston Hughes and Jean Toomer for their magnificent poetry. Ralph Ellison and James Baldwin are always sources when I get stuck. But really, one American writer, more than any, has been my bailiwick, my guiding light, my signpost.

OW: I think I know who you're going to say . . .

TM: It's Neal Pollack.

OW: Naturally.

TM: I read *Leon: A Man of the Streets* when I was just starting out as a writer, and I simply couldn't believe it. Here was a novel by a white man that captured African-American life in all its mess, its joy, its tragedy. He got the language right, he got the setting right, he got the humor right. There was not a moment of con-descension anywhere, and the book had a strong moral compass and sense of social justice without resorting to Richard Wright's unfocused anger.

OW: I know. I felt the exact same way when I read it. Well, Toni, what would you say if I told you that Neal Pollack himself was waiting backstage, and that he was going to join us right here, right now?

TM: I would say, "Girlfriend, bring him on!"

OW: Ladies and gentlemen, Neal Pollack!

[Two minutes of ear-splitting applause.]

OW: Neal, it is so wonderful to have you here.

NEAL POLLACK: Always a pleasure, my dear.

OW: You know Toni Morrison?

NP: Certainly. You look splendid, Ms. Morrison.

TM: You are looking fine yourself. I haven't seen you since . . . when was it? I think 1974.

NP: Yes. You were my editor for *The Creeping Madness and Other Tales of Equatorial Life.*

TM: That book was so fabulous! I barely changed a comma. Since then, I have simply worshiped you and everything you have ever done. I couldn't believe "I Am Friends with a Working-Class Black Woman." That was so right on the money. I thought it was the best thing written about welfare reform to date.

NP: Well, we must form a mutual admiration society. I almost quit writing forever after I read *Beloved,* and I still love *The Pinkest Eye . . .*

TM: *The Bluest Eye.*

NP: Yes, yes, of course. My goodness, Toni, you are a beautiful woman!

TM: Oh, my!

OW: Now, you two. Save that for after the show. Right now we have another special treat for you all. Joining us by satellite from Boston is Henry Louis Gates Jr., renowned author and the W. E. B. DuBois Professor of African-American Studies at Harvard University. Professor Gates, welcome.

HENRY LOUIS GATES JR.: Thank you, Oprah. Hello, there, Toni. And Mr. Pollack, it is a special honor to speak with you again.

NP: Thank you, Skip.

OW: Now, Professor Gates, since we have you for a short time only, and since we are blessed with Neal Pollack's presence here in the studio, perhaps you can talk a little about his influence on African-American writers like Toni Morrison.

HLGJR: Of course. Well, Oprah, as you know, I wrote a book called *Thirteen Ways of Looking at a Black Man,* which was well received and won several major honors. But at night, sleep wouldn't come to me. I felt that I had missed something in that book, something permanent and important. Then I realized the problem. There are actually fourteen ways of looking at a black man. I had forgotten about the best way, the most important way. Neal Pollack's way.

OW: Neal, perhaps you'd like to comment on what Toni Morrison and Henry Louis Gates Jr. have said about your writing. Why do you think you are the foremost interpreter of African-American culture today?

NP: I was talking about this the other day with Stanley Crouch and Wynton Marsalis. As usual, they were praising me to the heavens. Finally, I said to them, "Gentlemen, it is quite simple. I just write what I see." Now, perhaps I see more clearly than the ordinary person, but my books are still just the observations of one man on one planet at one pathetic moment in the history of the universe.

HLGJR: But what observations!

OW: Yes!

TM: Absolutely!

OW: Neal Pollack, don't go anywhere.

NP: I wouldn't dare. I've just begun to seduce Toni Morrison.

TM: Tee-hee.

OW: We'll be right back.

MY WEEK AT SEA

One morning in late August I stood on a platform in South Florida and stared at the hungry maw of the sea. My boots were rubber, my T-shirt cotton. The dock was wood, hard wood, tide-resistant, nut-brown wood. As I munched on a banana, a ripe, yellow banana, my knees trembled with the knowledge that this could be my last food until lunch. How I gazed at that water! How I longed to understand the secrets of its indifferent wetness! Oh!

The sea is immense, as are the creatures that skulk beneath its deceptively tranquil surface. Indeed, no man can fully understand our vast, enigmatic oceans, which cover at least 40 percent of the earth's surface, if not more. Sometimes there are waves, and then Lord save the man who doesn't own a Boogie board.

Think of all the men who've died at sea. Were they drunk when it happened? Were they stoned? Did they clutch one another, or shiver unaccompanied, afraid of what a goodbye hug might mean in the eyes of their harsh, bigoted god? Who were these noble, air-dried souls who gave their lives in exchange for a scintilla of insight into the mysteries of the infinite deep?

Hard to say. That's why I was in Florida on an assignment from a major American magazine, looking for a ship, preferably one with a decent kitchen. If I found a really great vessel, one with quirky characters and the possibility for melodrama, maybe

I could also get a book contract. Also, I thought, snorkeling equipment would be nice.

I inhaled the roiling surf, the cresting tide of that cruel mistress, the sea. My illusions were few. I knew she would cheat on me as well, but I was ready for her faithless ways.

"Bring it on, sea!" I shouted into the surprisingly mild wind. "Bring it on!"

THE SCOOBY II, in seafarers' terms, is a dumpy little glass-bottomed sloop generally used for touristic purposes. A cooler containing seven cases of beer sits on her back deck, and she also boasts a portable cassette machine that continually plays Bob Marley's *Legend* album. She's inexpensive to rent for the week, which is important if one wishes to go to sea on a per-diem voucher. A dancing, top-hat-wearing cartoon octopus is painted on her bow.

The boat's skipper is a salty, crusty old salt who wears a permanent leer and constantly chews on the back end of a candle. He has a scar, a half-inch in diameter, that runs from the nape of his neck down to the nape of his pelvis, taking a sharp turn in the vicinity of his chest and wrapping around his back. It also runs down his right leg, making it hard to tell where the scar begins and where it ends.

"Let me guess," I say. "You were battling a swordfish, ten fathoms deep, on the bounds of a three-hundred-foot drop-off near a coral reef. That fish wrenched your line and rode it a mile. Your hook flew loose and ripped you in half."

"Nope," says the captain.

His name is Marion Motley.

"Didn't you once play fullback for the Cleveland Browns?" I ask.

"Nope," he says.

Also on board the *Scooby II* is the cook, a fleshy Guatemalan named Miguel. At sea, you are invariably faced with inner torment and self-loathing. All your mistakes raise up every night, like Poseidon, and stab you in the face with a spear, so any food is a delicious relief. Miguel makes Stouffer's French Bread Pizza and Hungry Man Salisbury Steak with Mashed Potatoes, and I feel good.

On the second night, after we have putzed around a lagoon, floated on rafts, and gotten plowed on the deck, another member of the crew appears, brawny and silent. He is the color of bronze. His nipples are pierced with golden loops. He wears nothing but a loincloth and an elaborate head decoration of a snarling wolf. This is connected to a long strip of fur, which runs down his back.

"Why is he dressed like that?" I ask the captain.

"Because," the captain says, "he is a Native American."

I HAVE BROUGHT along sea literature for my journey: *Moby-Dick,* Poe's *The Narrative of Arthur Gordon Pym,* and *One Fish, Two Fish, Red Fish, Blue Fish.*

I lie reading on the deck. An expansive, feathery shadow casts itself over my ever-learning form. I look above. A bird.

I have had several beers.

"It is the mighty albatross!" I shout.

But it is only a pelican, and I quickly take a nap.

ON THE MORNING of the fourth day, the *Scooby II* docks at the Caribbean island of St. Walter. Here we pick up the captain's wife, a magnificently proportioned twenty-two-year-old Tejana law student named Lucia. Tejanas have been fishing the Caribbean for decades, maybe even longer. But very few know how to fish like Lucia. She is a Special Fisherwoman. Her technique alone is worth a paragraph.

She turns in a circle three times and pulls a worm from her wallet. She swallows the worm and sticks a shrimp, peeled, on her hook instead. Then she attaches the hook—which is sharp—to the line, and throws the whole thing in the water, first making sure that the line is attached to a pole. Afterward, she waits. If a fish bites, she reels it in. Wow.

On this trip, she will not be fishing, because she has a tort exam on Tuesday.

"Oh, come on!" I say.

"Shut up," says the captain.

That night, I eat a Lean Cuisine prepared by Miguel. Later, he and I play Scrabble, which I win handily, since he doesn't speak English. I go to my bunk and try to sleep. I can hear that Captain Motley and Lucia are having guttural, desperate sex in the cabin above.

My brain shivers with restless desire. Sex at sea is something I have never experienced. I once had sex in a swimming pool, with a political consultant named Lindsey. But that was at the 1972 Democratic National Convention.

ON THE SIXTH day, it rains. The wind blows at speeds of ten to fifteen miles an hour. The waves are several feet high.

We are belowdecks, playing Uno. I am bored and I want to experience the tumult of the sea.

I toss down my cards, even though I am holding several Draw Fours.

"Take me, sea!" I shout. "Take me in your arms!"

The Native American is standing on the bow, staring at the clouded heavens. He motions to the water.

"Jump in," he says.

They are the first words he has uttered all week, and they are correct. The air is quiet, uneasily so, like quiet air. The ocean, four feet below me, looks like the landscape of another planet, one with turtles. The Native American looks at me, then looks away, then looks at me again. He is creeping me out.

My knees end and my legs rise. I don't remember telling them to do this. For a second, my body is in the air. Then it's not. It accelerates, slows down. It is dry. Then, it's wet. Suddenly, I have no past, no present, and no future. I am just a writer bobbing in the middle of the sea. For the first time since the voyage started, I reflect on my own death.

Then it is over. The Native American throws a rope ladder into the water, and I am on deck.

"Can I have a towel?" I say. "Please?"

He looks at me sadly, as though I have learned an important lesson too young, too soon. And I have, because the sea is not about adventure, or finding your manhood. No. The sea is alive, it is very sad, and everything about it makes me want to go home and watch TV.

SOON, THE VOYAGE ends. I say goodbye and hand the captain a large check, at which he barely grunts. The weariness in my bones can only be matched by the heaviness in my heart. Oh, sorrowful sea.

I strap on my backpack, heave over the boat's side, and begin walking down the dock to a fading strain of Bob Marley music.

No one waves goodbye.

Then, an explosion that is loud followed by a wave of heat. I turn around, notebook already drawn. The *Scooby II* is immersed in fire.

"Sweet Jesus and Mary save us!" someone screams.

The cartoon octopus melts away. The mast crackles and falls. The bow splits in twain, and so does the stern. Yet still the Prophet echoes from deep within the inner cabin.

Exodus, movement of the people . . .

Captain Marion Motley appears in the chaos, holding the lifeless body of his trophy wife.

"Dear Lord, why?" he shouts.

The unholy fire straddles his heels, then consumes him as well.

You can't fool all the people all the time . . .

I feel that I should go for help, as these people are clearly anguished. After all, I am clear of the boat, and will certainly survive. But I am too busy taking notes. A book idea has come to me; I have participated in the last voyage of the *Scooby II* and lived to tell its story. I will owe an immense debt, if not any actual residual money, to the people who died so my book could be brought into the world.

An hour later, upon the scene are police and firefighters and the lesser media, who don't have the depth of knowledge about this tragedy that I do. They will file their reports and move onto the next disaster, but I will construct a narrative unlike any the publishing world has ever witnessed.

The sun descends in the cruel, cruel west. A furry wolf's head bobs to the surface of the water, and I realize the enormity of the loss. Another silent Native American has been consumed by the eternal Atlantic. What a way to go. I walk down the beach, shoes off, talking into a tape recorder. My feet snag on what appears to be a small piece of cloth, but is actually a large piece of cloth. Oh, no. It's Miguel's chef apron.

The poor fellow, I think. He was awfully heavy, and the captain often kept him chained to his bunk. He must have sunk like a boulder. I remember the last conversation we had, as I taught him multiplication at midnight, using flash cards.

"This voyage has been the fulfillment of all my dreams," he said. "I cannot wait to visit my family in Chichicastenango and tell them I got to meet an actual American journalist."

People often react this way to me.

"What else will you say to them?" I sighed, knowing what I would hear.

"That your credentials were excellent," he said. "and you are such a handsome, handsome man!"

(From *The Creeping Madness and Other Tales of Equatorial Life,* 1974)

BLURBS*

"Like a star shining in the night, but brighter, this book illumines the human condition like no other. With wit and quiet intelligence, Pollack delineates the fine line between good and evil that we all must daily walk. . . . He truly is a contemporary master."

—Annie Dillard

"Neal Pollack is the Pollack's Pollack, the trickster monkey of our souls. He is a rat bastard and he owes me money. He is also the greatest living American writer, and the *Anthology* proves it, the fucker."

—Hunter S. Thompson, ESPN.com

---

*Author's note: It was originally my intent to include all these blurbs, most of which are from my friends, colleagues, and former and current lovers, at the front of the book. But because of the recent economic downturn, which has, among other tragedies, increased the rate of returns from big chain bookstores, I have graciously agreed to downplay my popularity to allow other HarperCollins authors a fighting chance in this narrow market. After all, if the midlist rises, those of us at the top of the list float higher as well. So instead, we are footnoting these blurbs, since they are, after all, important and instructive. Also, the lawyers told us we'd get sued if we led with them. So here we are. Enjoy.

"Through careful, balanced reporting, Pollack captures the tensions of urban life with unfailing accuracy and sympathy. The *Anthology* works on eighteen different levels—as sociology, journalism, history, and epic narrative, among others. A profound reimagining of our national character . . . a spectacular masterpiece."

—Nicholas Lemann, *The Atlantic Monthly*

"An erotic thriller that far surpasses the best work of other erotic thriller writers. Sexually complex, but always generous, Pollack is remapping the landscape of human passion and romantic possibility. No author alive creates more complex women. The *Anthology* . . . is a great leap forward in literary onanism. How does he do it?"

—Robert Olen Butler

"Fascinating . . . Pollack's portrait of turn-of-the-century New York is both calculated and deeply moving, but never disingenuous. His urban landscape dances with life."

—Luc Sante, *Dissent*

"A grim recitation of every imaginable societal illness . . . darkly hilarious."

—James Wood, *The New Republic*

"As in his previous trilogy of Indian novels, *The Mango in the Guava Tree, Big Trouble in the Betel Orchard of Small Things,* and *A Suitable Ghee,* Pollack captures the sweet, bitter realities of life on the Subcontinent."

—Ruth Prawer Jhabvala

"At last, an honest book from the source! Pollack may be just the man to save hip-hop from itself."

—Russell Simmons

"An unparalleled treasury of wonder . . . This book lands Pollack in a small category (Kafka, Joyce, and Shakespeare come to mind), of writers who tower above all humanity in their bigness. Pollack is more than a cunning stylist. His stories both transcend and re-create reality in the spirit of our time."

—Isabel Allende, *Boston Globe*

"The best book to come out of Latin America in the last fifty years."

—Sven Birkerts, *Los Angeles Times*

"Despite Pollack's age and great experience, he nonetheless manages to freshly chronicle the lives of contemporary young people in all their media-drenched messiness. Full of tricks but never false, Pollack is the old bard of a new generation."

—Douglas Coupland

"As a registered Democrat and a lapsed but hopeful feminist with an unlimited travel budget, I thoroughly enjoyed this book. Pollack is Sisyphus without the ball-rolling-down-the-hill bit. Like Diana in the forest, he is the bitch-goddess in all her bisexual splendor, the mother-cunt wide open to the world."

—Camille Paglia

"Pollack has reached the snow-capped peak of his destiny by laying bare the sexual hypocrisies of the American university. A book sure to be debated and masturbated over in the libraries of the Eastern seaboard . . . Pollack's *Anthology* is better than *Lolita*."

—Donna Tartt

"As the cloven-hoofed one's coming approaches, Pollack's work is a clarion call for all true patriots. A must-read for those of us who hear the infernal throb of the black helicopters."

—William H. Pierce, Ph.D., author, *The Turner Diaries*

"A profoundly comic work of deep seriousness."

—John Updike, *Golf Digest*

"From the anti-sweatshop campaign at the University of Michigan to the struggle to unionize teaching assistants at Yale to the busloads of students who attended the WTO protests in Seattle, the Left is alive and well on American college campuses."

—*The Nation*

"Pollack is the foremost chronicler of the African-American experience."

—Henry Louis Gates Jr.

"A kind-hearted balladeer's vision of small-town America. The voices in this book rise to an unbearably happy chorus that spreads over the plains and penetrates our hearts. A fresh mushroom sprouting from the virgin grass at dawn . . . Pure storytelling at its finest."

—Verlyn Klinkenborg, *Utne Reader*

"Reminiscent of Poe and Chekhov, yet with Melvillian breadth. Pollack weaves a world as memorable as that of Dickens, but with the broad scatological scope of *South Park* and *The Simpsons*."

—*The Oxford American*

"Like Balzac, Pollack has created a living, breathing world in its totality. In this case, however, his setting is not the garrets of Paris, but the northern New Jersey suburbs, his human backdrop not bohemia, but the white-hot, and very real, American Mafia. Pollack alternately horrifies and seduces the reader, with a supporting cast that we grow to love even as he whacks them and throws them into the trunk of his Cadillac. At the book's center are the sexually charged scenes between Pollack and his Italian-American psychiatrist. Never has dramatic tension been made so palpably honest. Bada-bing!"

—*US Magazine*

"I have seen the new face of horror, and its name is Neal Pollack."

—Stephen King

LETTER FROM PARIS

Paris is lovely, from my perspective. In all, I have spent three months in this greatest of cities, this shadowy, prodigious place of grand boulevards and crusty, delicious bread, and I feel compelled to record my impressions. The French are so French, so alien, so very unlike any other people on earth. This being France, and me being an American, I am humdrum, inferior to their imposing food, their unusual plumbing, their fat but somehow sophisticated cows. Yet for their own enigmatic reasons, the French have embraced me, and hard. I am the most toasted dinner guest in the Sixteenth Arrondisement. My comprehension of the culture astonishes even the most jaded observers. No one says "feh" in my presence, not here anyway. I am not your average American in Paris, no naïf, and no inexperienced rube. I am the world's most sophisticated traveler. Still, what does Paris, glorious Paris, care about that? I can't promise to reveal to you *the* Paris, only *my* Paris, a Paris I have discovered and grown to adore. It is a partial Paris, an incomplete Paris, but a Paris nonetheless. So come then, my friend. Join me in my discoveries. Come. Come to Paris with me.

I FELT LIKE a stranger my first few weeks here, much stranger than Camus could have even imagined, back in his novel-writing days. I was being paid by several publications to chronicle my adjustment, but initially, I didn't speak a word of French, which created some difficulties.

Upon arriving in Paris, I didn't eat for the first two days. I merely wandered the streets, famished and exhausted, clutching my stomach in agony and longingly staring at the pastry-filled windows. I briefly thought of stealing a loaf of bread, like Jean Valjean in *Les Misérables,* which I was soon to read in the original French and understand completely. Then I realized my starvation was absurd since I had a thousand dollars in my front pocket and another two thousand in my luggage, which I'd stashed in a storage locker at the train station until I could figure out where I was going to stay.

But as I walked into restaurant after restaurant, waving my American dollars, no one would serve me. I thought for certain that I'd gone insane. On my third day in Paris, crazed from hunger, I stopped a portly man who was wearing an American-flag hat and T-shirt bearing the likeness of Richard Petty, the prominent race-car driver. He explained to me that I needed to exchange my money into francs, and then I would be able to eat. Well, who knew? Later I found out that soon France would be getting a whole new currency, called the *euro,* which many other European countries would also use. Personally, I don't see why they all can't use the American dollar, but I suppose it's none of my business.

Soon after exchanging my money into "francs," I wandered into an attractive-looking establishment with red-leather bar stools and a zinc countertop. Unfortunately, as usual, the waiter didn't speak English, but I communicated to him what I wanted by rubbing my stomach and clawing insanely at my bloodshot eyes. He brought me a fried-egg sandwich and a Coca-Cola. In all, the meal only cost me seventeen dollars.

BEFORE MY PARISIAN golden age began, I had trouble meeting actual French people, since there weren't many around the Eiffel Tower, except for the hundreds of small, looming men at the base who attempted to sell me a variety of wind-up dancing animals. In fact, the majority of people at the Tower seemed to be Japanese. In the elevator up to the top, I met two young women from Holland. They asked me where I was from.

"Bonjour," I said, using my nascent language skills. "I am from France."

I stooped, and squinted an eye.

"Would you like to buy a wind-up monkey?" I said.

They laughed suggestively, and informed me that they were both named Anabel. When they asked me where I was staying, I told them I'd been living on the street for the last week because I couldn't figure out where any of the hotels were.

"You need to come stay at the youth hostel with us," said an Anabel, and she winked at me with lusty intention.

This is great, I thought. I've only been in Paris a week, and now I'm going to have sex with two women named Anabel, from Holland.

As we headed back to the elevators, we were swarmed by an enormous crush of Japanese, who pushed Anabel and Anabel ahead of me into a full compartment. I shouted for them to wait, but when I got to the bottom, they were gone.

I DECIDED THAT I needed a French teacher. At a café one day, I asked the first big-breasted woman I saw if she would help me.

"Non," she said. But I produced a folder that contained carefully chosen excerpts from the latest reviews of my novel, and she relented. Her doubting eyes soon became churning pools of desire.

Later, as a soothing breeze blew over our entwined bodies, she said, "The first sentence you must learn is 'Tu es parfait.'"

What that meant, exactly, I didn't know, but I could guess. Perfection is the same in every language.

I had traveled far since my early weeks in Paris, when my near miss with the Anabels had left me in a state of extreme sexual restlessness. In those early, non-puissant days, I could find no way to quench my desires in a city full of love.

I wandered to the neighborhood of Montmartre, where I

heard writers and painters had once lived. Perhaps, I thought, this would be a good place for *l'amour*. When I arrived, I boarded "The Little Train of Montmartre," which had a tour guide who spoke English.

As the trolley meandered through the streets, our guide pointed out a series of uninteresting buildings. My attention was instead riveted on the great variety of sex shops lining the neighborhood's main thoroughfares. Swarthy, eager-looking men beckoned and leered, thrusting flyers into my hands as the train crawled past. Many of the signs were in English. They advertised such exotica as "XXX Floor Shows," "Beautiful Dancing Women," and "Hot Polish Ladies." The opportunities for erotic fulfillment seemed limitless, and my stomach began to churn and well.

Lust rose up like a snarling beast, and filled my head with a strange buzzing. This was madness, but then, as I have learned, what is Paris but a fabulous, collective madness, with excellent liqueurs available twenty-four hours?

I tore from the bus and snatched a one-franc coin from my wallet. Within seconds, I had entered a public toilet, where I sought sweet relief from the terrible desires that were coursing through my skull. Paris had finally, fully, worked its strange, obscure magic on me, as it had on so many young men before. It was a moment for which I had traveled a long, long way.

"Oh! Paris!" I shouted. "My Paris! Beautiful, magical city of lights!"

(From *Europe: The Forgotten Continent,* 1951)

A COUNTRY HOUSE
IN THE COUNTRY

America, as I have often stated in my essays and at various luncheons for which I receive speaking honoraria, is a land of competing desires. We want to live in a city, to be part of the grand pageant of gunning down immigrants, kicking old ladies out of their apartments, and hanging out in candlelit bars with private couch alcoves. But we also want to live in the country, because the land calls us; in a three-part harmony, it is singing our name from the damp, fertile loam. Indeed, this national dichotomy goes all the way back. The city was Hamilton. The country was Jefferson. There was also once a third option, but that vanished with the Lincoln assassination, which I chronicled in my recent historical novel *The Incredibly True Tale of the Brief History of the Story of John Wilkes Booth.*

As America's leading naturalist with a multibook deal, I have always wanted to write on this topic. Who knows the landscape better, after all? Wallace Stegner is dead, so is Edward Abbey, and Wendell Berry is old. So I bought a house in Vermont. What follows is excerpted from *Memories of Logan County,* my forthcoming account of the year I spent there. They were days of joy, but also pain. Sunshine, and rain. You're not invited to visit, but through the magic of the artificial diary device, I now implore you to join me. Friends, nature calls. Welcome to a year at my country house.

JUNE 7

Woke at 6 A.M. to find a patch of daisies growing beneath my bedroom window. I drew the curtain closed immediately, as Charlize Theron and I had been up all night doing whippets. The sound of an electric saw in the distance was heard. "Shut the fuck up!" I shouted. "Arrrgh!"

JUNE 12

Stopped by the seed store to inquire about the possibility of having someone come up the hill to repair my cappuccino maker. "Williams-Sonoma won't deliver replacement parts," I said. "Can you believe it?" "Nope," said the counterman. Later, an eave chipped. Isn't that charming?

JUNE 15

At night, I can hear the trees sing to me. At day, I nap.

JUNE 17

Thought about building a barn. Had no idea where I could get some wood. Also, I needed an ax. The whole enterprise eventually made me sad, so I drank a lot of wine.

JULY 3

Served as Grand Marshal for Logan County Days and gave a pep talk to the junior twirling squad, which turned me on, unnaturally. I stanched my lust with a brief, barely legal dalliance under the junior-college float. Afterward, I roasted a pig in my backyard. The caterers overcharged me for tapenade.

JULY 9

A shapeless, horrible man-thing haunts these woods. It goes by many names: Sasquatch, the White Beast, Elwood, the Thief of

Hearts. I can feel it out there, watching me with its eyes, waiting to pounce. I listen to Springsteen, but he provides little protection, and my soul is chilled with eternal fear. Death stalks me, waiting to consume my flesh.

July 22

Hot tub installed.

August 15

My house is suffering from exploding casements. I have never heard of a casement, and I have to look it up in the dictionary. After receiving replacement bids from several shutter manufacturers, I wonder: What has become of me? Then I smell the air, and I realize that I have changed forever. A pity that the fall literary festivals start soon, and I won't be able to return until ski season.

December 6

Winter has settled over the land, covering the land with a thick blanket of winter. I invite friends from the city for a retro fondue party. We wear sweaters, dip our sour apples, and listen to records. The shapeless thing watches from the woods, and I can hear its whisper on the winds. "Gruyère," it moans, "Gruyère . . ."

April 7

This year, I will plant marijuana, for medicinal purposes. It is my duty as a man and a farmer, and I'm going to make a lot of money, too. There is no way that the Supreme Court will ever make it illegal. Not now. We've come too far as a society. I hork a bong and feel good about myself.

May 3

My no-good son-in-law comes to visit and ends up with his ass sticking out of a pile of hay. Also, he crashes a crop duster into the greenhouse and accidentally feeds arsenic to the goat. When will his wacky antics cease?

MAY 28

I am reading by the pond when I hear a rustling, and I know that the woods have, at last, come to claim me. I close my eyes and prepare for the devouring. The beast emerges, and he is filthy, his bulbous head covered with matted leaves, his legs distended into a hideous parody of distension. I recognize him instantly.

"So, it's you, Salinger," I say. "At last."

He emits a deep, terrifying howl of the lost.

"What do you have to say for yourself?" I ask.

"Please," he croaks, "can I have some spicy turkey sausage?"

So I cook dinner, one recluse for another, and it is delicious. Our hunger is sated, our loneliness solved, and the mysteries of nature vanish like the wind. I feel like we could talk forever, or at least for a couple of hours.

JUNE 2

I begin work on my book *Salinger: Man-Creature of Vermont,* which has been nominated in advance for the Pulitzer Prize. The proceeds from the book, I announce in a press conference, will go toward the purchase of a better house.

(From *A Seed in the Garden: The Collected Nature Writing of Neal Pollack,* 1980)

I HAVE SLEPT WITH
FIVE HUNDRED WOMEN

In the spring of 1983, Sarah Lawrence College asked me to address its graduating seniors. I was already doing three other commencement speeches that weekend, but I agreed because the college offered me several thousand dollars and an ample supply of rum and painkillers. I worked on the speech for at least an hour, but couldn't come up with a single original sentiment. So I just showed up and talked. What spontaneously emerged was brilliant almost beyond imagination. The text follows.

Perhaps you think that it would be easy for me, an Ivy League graduate and published novelist who has a good-paying day job at a major television network, to find true love. But it is not. I have searched everywhere—Chicago, San Francisco, Seattle, Paris, Rome, and even, on occasion, Brooklyn—for the woman who can fully understand my unique branded mix of wistful intelligence and mild, but endearing, neurotic tics. This woman should also like cats, because I cherish them so much.

But nothing has emerged; I have found no love, no one with whom to share my life.

Instead, all I have found is sex, and nothing but. I have slept with five hundred women, maybe more, but certainly not fewer. No matter where I go, no matter what the occasion, I always end up having sexual intercourse with some woman. They are usually beautiful, intelligent, charming, and sophisticated. They generally think I'm pretty hot. We often delight in the curves of each other's bodies. We always fuck like wildebeest.

But we never fall in love.

Just last night, for instance, I was at a party thrown by the chief editor at a major publishing house, who happens to be a good friend of mine. I hadn't been there five minutes when I fell into conversation with a sleek, black-haired beauty, a prize-winning poet and ranking business executive who is also the director of a folkloric music festival in her native country of Peru. Sure enough, within an hour, we were fuckin'!

This morning, I turned to her and said, "Do you think . . . we could ever fall in love with each other?"

"Love is for fools," she said. "Ram me again, you hot stud! Ram me all day long!"

My diet of unhindered sexual pleasure grows less nourishing every day. Sometimes, I am plunged into depressions that cannot be cured, not even by massive doses of Valium. When I'm on assignment in, say, Turkey, and the women of Istanbul are launching themselves at me like rockets, I want to scream, "Por favor! Dejame! Leave me alone!" But I don't, and soon enough I'm trapped once again in the pit of knives that more naive men call "the sack." At times, only the slim, ephemeral dream that I will someday fall in love keeps me from shuffling off this wretched, tormented, sex-filled mortal coil.

I am tired of being propositioned on airplanes. I cannot tell you how many times I've been forced into illicit sex in public toilets. One grows tired of having an opera singer grinding on one's face while a conceptual artist sucks mightily between one's legs. It loses its charm.

Enough of sex! Enough fellatio! Do you hear me, people of the world? I don't want to fuck you anymore! I only want your love. Love me, dammit, love me! Love, love, love! People of the world, hear my cry! I am your hobbyhorse no more!

INTRODUCTION TO THE
NEW SLAVERY

My handsome and wealthy friend David, who is half Jamaican, works for NBC. He has published a collection of short stories set in Scotland, and is working on another collection, set in Wales. On average, he makes love to three different women a week. Yet he is unhappy. Recently, I visited him in his East Village duplex, and he explained why.

He stood in his sunken living room wearing nothing but a pair of fuzzy brown shorts, a platinum nipple ring,* and a bowler

---

*Unlike in my critical heyday, when magazines small and large such as *The American Century, The Left of Left Review,* and Walter Winchell's *Books at Sea* carried on important debates vital to the republic, in today's limp and flatulent literary environment, critics are afraid to criticize and writers are afraid to write, mostly for fear of not having anyone to talk to at cocktail parties. This essential cowardice, combined with massive corporate consolidation of the publishing industry (which prevents younger writers with lesser reputations than mine from getting their feet in the proverbial door), one publication stands as the arbiter of all taste and judgment: the *New York Times Book Review.* Naturally, they get everything wrong. So recently, I decided to take them on in public. It was a bold move, even a stupid one. But I sold thousands and thousands of books and got free drugs during a speaking engagement on the island of Ibiza. Here now, in footnote form, we present the original review, by a talented know-nothing named Shafer, hat. In this age, where online jobs appear and disappear like fairies in a howling wind, where nothing is what it seems, where

———————————

(continued)

followed by my correction, which ran in the *Wall Street Journal*'s weekend Books section. I hope you squint and find it instructive.

THE REVIEW
BY JACK SHAFER

To paraphrase Oscar Levant, there's a thin line between good writing and bad writing, and Neal Pollack erases it forever with *The Neal Pollack Anthology of American Literature,* his flippant sendup of the literary elite. The proudly callow Neal Pollack of the byline, a thirty-something who was most recently a writer at *The Chicago Reader,* has imagined the entire corpus of a name-dropping, self-aggrandizing, oversexed litterateur, also named Neal Pollack. "When I'm on assignment in, say, Turkey . . . the women of Istanbul are launching themselves at me like rockets," Pollack writes. "Salinger, as you know, was once a great writer like myself," he says elsewhere. This fictional Pollack—a graduate of Exeter and Harvard, now in his seventies—considers himself the greatest magazine journalist, novelist, and poet in the history of American letters, not to mention a helluva radio producer. He collects Pulitzers, Bookers, and National Book Awards the way furniture collects dust.

The anthology's twenty-four short "excerpts" from seven decades of the fictional Pollack's journalism serve to parody the genre of literary journalism, and the joke proves surprisingly durable given its narrow premise. At first glance, Pollack's model seems to be Gore Vidal. The fictional Pollack slums in Hollywood as a screenwriter before getting blacklisted; he keeps a summer estate in Malta; he pines for his murdered Exeter roommate, Wally Trumbull, the way Vidal does in his memoir *Palimpsest* for his lost boyhood love, Jimmie Trimble. Pollack writes, "All my inspiration is derived from a solitary source: a waking, eternal longing to once again hold Wally Trumbull . . . in my tanned and muscular arms. I remember the first night we lay together, the bagels aren't even warm anymore, really, coherent clothing choices don't apply.

(continued)

moonlight reflecting off his Captain America pajama bottoms, his hairless chest glistening with the tender sweat of youth."

But Pollack's target isn't just Vidal. He's drawn a bead on every high-paid magazine writer and alpha-male novelist to swagger through the pages of *GQ, Esquire,* or *Rolling Stone;* every *New Yorker* or *Vanity Fair* puffer fish to file first-person, ego-enriched letters from exotic datelines; every overwriter interviewed by *The Paris Review.* Think Norman Mailer. John Gregory Dunne. Christopher Hitchens. Gay Talese. Michael Herr. Mike Sager. Truman Capote. Peter Matthiessen. Martin Amis. Think Norman Mailer again.

Deftly ridiculing these masters of the form, Pollack forever soils the genre of literary journalism for even lesser voices. I defy anybody to read Sebastian Junger with a straight face after consuming "The Albania of My Existence," the first entry here: "I've been going to bed lately on a pile of jagged stones covered only by a thin cotton blanket half-eaten by moths. . . . I have personally borne witness to much human suffering. People here are beset by unwanted refugees, obscure diseases, and limited opportunities to express themselves through fashion. I must tell you: things are not good."

The fictional Pollack shares a meal of dirt with the impoverished locals, watches as "the village children play soccer with the bloated carcass of a cat" and then looks on as a mob impales a man on a stake in the town square. "I want to ask: for what crime was this man sentenced to die? But I do not speak Albanian." Packing his bags, he muses about the human calamity that would mean nothing if not channeled through Pollack, the weary foreign correspondent: "I cry silent tears, and pray for the people of this sorrow-ridden country, and for myself." The only cliché that's missing is the ethnic music they cue at the end of a foreign dispatch on NPR's *All Things Considered.*

This collection takes an efficient swipe at white liberal writers who cruise the projects looking for story subjects in "I Am Friends

"I want a slave," he said.

"What?"

"Life has failed me. Despite my immense good fortune, good looks, and tasty collection of imported cheeses, it is getting

---

(continued)

with a Working-Class Black Woman" and Hemingway pretenders in "Portrait of an Andalusian Horse Trainer": "The colt loomed monstrously in front of a swirling wall of rain clouds. He was El Caballo de Sangre, the Horse of Blood, the death horse." (The book's sly "Publishing Notes" claim that the piece originally appeared in *The Saturday Evening Post* as "I Get a Kick Out of You, Spain.") In "Interlude: The Pollack-Wilson Letters," Edmund Wilson concedes that Pollack is his better. "Your life of Tocqueville is remarkable, as is your recent trilogy of short novels about Cambodia," the ailing dean of American literature writes, confiding in a letter that begins "Dearest Nealster" that his last book will be about Pollack "and the friendship that we have shared."

If I read the young Pollack right, he means more than to cripple hacks with the mace of parody. Like Dave Eggers and the other literary monkey-wrenchers at *McSweeney's Quarterly,* where some of these pieces first appeared and which published this book, Pollack longs to make literary noise of his own. But first he must vanquish the practitioners of a school of journalism that substitutes a dilettante's superficial experience for genuine reporting. Or maybe Pollack just wants to have fun drawing silly mustaches on famous writers.

Alas, the art of silly-mustache drawing—maestros like Woody Allen and Bruce McCall will tell you—is a minimalist one. Whenever Pollack extends the joke much beyond 600 words, the effect wanes. Try as I might, I couldn't find the laughs in "Teenagers: The Enemy Within," the book's longest piece, an ostensible investigation of "the secret world of teenagers," or "The Subcomandante Rides at Dawn," a longish "dispatch" from Chiapas. Generous readers will give Pollack credit for attempting to sustain the preening persona of his alter ego at book length. But stingy readers, having gotten the book's joke halfway through, harder and harder for me to feel like a whole human being. Religion doesn't appeal, and politics are in spiral decline. Science is interesting, but who has the time to understand it? I can't even comprehend the weather anymore. I make up for my cognitive

---

(*continued*)

    will ask why Pollack squanders his comic gifts with writing that is
    every bit as self-indulgent as the bloviations he wants to take down.

THE CORRECTION

DATE: March 13, 2001
PERIODICAL: *New York Times Book Review*
AUTHOR: Jack Shafer, deputy editor, *Slate*
CLARIFICATION BY: Neal Pollack

With sales of my book nearing one million copies, I should not feel obligated to publish this corrective. But as a journalist myself, I am committed to accuracy, even if professional blood has to be shed, even if the dogs of my competitive spirit tear at the rotting corpses of my literary lessers, those who wish to ridicule and destroy me. I have never met Mr. Shafer, nor have I read *Slate* or the *New York Times Book Review,* as I tend to ignore all English-language periodicals unless they are published in India or contain pictures of Lucy Lawless. Still, I cannot believe that editors with professional degrees, even ones who work for publications in severe financial distress, would allow such shoddy reviewing to occur.

Let me, then, reclaim my reputation. First, I am not, as Mr. Shafer claims, a "pedophile with a heart of gold." At least not anymore, and any such rumors have long since been buried through massive payoffs and brass-knuckle beatings. Second, my mother does not operate a "Tijuana gin joint." Her bar is, in fact, in Nogales, Arizona, and she has never served gin. Other, more minor mistakes in this review also harm my reputation. My book has not yet been published in Hungary, I did not play the Cookie Monster in "Sesame Street on Ice," and I did not appear as a character named "Frankie Boner" on the first season of *The Sopranos.* Where you got such information, Jack, is beyond me, but Jesus

deficiencies by drinking heavily, or having sex with the door-
man's wife. But these are fleeting pleasures."

I felt vaguely ill, like the time my ex-girlfriend's brother was
brutally murdered by a sadistic graduate student at Yale. But as

---

(continued)

> Christ, man. You could have asked me during our E-mail correspon-
> dence, which I reprint here.
>
> Also, I think you misinterpreted my book entirely. This is a serious
> work of fiction and nonfiction and poetry, not a collection of parodies. I
> am not sure from whence you gleaned the parodic intent, but let me
> assure you that everything I have ever said and done my entire life,
> including appearing on *Hollywood Squares,* has been with pure sincerity. I
> know you more or less liked the book, but it is a matter of tone, Jack,
> and intent, and you have obviously failed to grasp every subtlety of my
> work. I would have rather you hated the book, Jack, than have told the
> readers of the *New York Times Book Review* that I was "the funniest Amer-
> ican since Groucho Marx, and even then, almost funnier." Not fair, pal.
>
> Thank you for understanding. I know that you are jealous of my success,
> and I hope my corrections will make you a better book reviewer. Hold
> them close to your heart like a boyhood doll you love, and you may still
> be able to salvage your career. I'll see you at the Montana Writers' Spa
> Weekend and Private Sex Retreat in July.
>
> Yours in the Revolution,
> NP

E-MAIL

> Subj: I'm reviewing your book
> Date: 2/28/01 11:04:49 AM US Eastern Standard Time
> From: Jack.Shafer@netzero.com (Jack Shafer)
> To: sillyrabbit305@aol.com (Neal Pollack)
>
> Neal:
>
> I'm reviewing your book for the *Times Book Review.* It should be pub-
> lished in a couple of weeks. I have one question: Did some of the pieces
> in the book originally appear in *McSweeney's?*

then, the feeling quickly passed, and I began to think about my own unhappiness.

"I must be someone's master," David said. "I must have a slave."

(continued)

> Subj: RE: I'm reviewing your book
> Date: 3/1/01 11:04:55 AM US Eastern Standard Time
> From: ilovebuffy@yahoo.com (Neal Pollack)
> To: jack@jack.net (Jack Shafer)
>
> Jack:
>
> Yes, they did. Thanks for telling me. I look forward to reading the review.

> Subj: One more question
> Date: 3/1/01 1:33:03 PM US Eastern Standard Time
> From: Sammysosafan@smithsonian.us.gov (Jack Shafer)
> To: Bluehighways@hotmail.com (Neal Pollack)
>
> Neal:
>
> How old are you?

> Subj: RE: One more question
> Date: 3/1/01 1:33:04 PM US Eastern Standard Time
> From: dudelookslikealady@aol.com (Neal Pollack)
> To: lornaluft@monster.com (Jack Shafer)
>
> Jack:
>
> I'm 31. Hey. One favor. Please don't use the word "bloviations" in your review. I hate that word.

> Subj: No problem
> Date: 3/1/01 1:33:05 PM US Eastern Standard Time
> From: deltaofvenus@ebay.com (Jack Shafer)
> To: agingbigman@aol.com (Patrick Ewing)
>
> OK. I hate that word too.

* * *

THE NEXT DAY, I saw a woman in my neighborhood wearing nothing but a bright red diaper, and it got me to thinking. One hundred, twenty, even five years ago, David's desire for slave ownership would have been viewed with suspicion, or possibly punished through imprisonment. But our social codes have changed, and our daily intercourse has changed as well. Work, like love, seems passé. The world has been reduced to a seemingly endless succession of consumer choices. We are bored by entertainment, and entertained by boredom. Why shouldn't we have slaves if we want them?

I took this question to my uncle Walter, who is a retired professor of metaphysics at New York University. Today, he and my aunt Sylvia live in a geodesic dome on Long Island. But when I was young, I used to go to their brownstone in Brooklyn, listen to the dog races on the radio, and poison pigeons on the roof. Those were days of meaning and coherence, even when they served me creamed cabbage for lunch.

"Uncle Walter," I said to him, "what do you think about reinstating slavery?"

He punched me in the gut, but it really didn't hurt. The exertion was too much for him, and he fell onto the floor, gasping.

"No man is another man's property," he croaked.

Idealism, I thought, how charmingly old-fashioned. After calling an ambulance, I popped in a Pavement CD and thought of the household items I'd recently purchased. There had been two matching end tables from Ikea, a Versace teacup and saucer set, and a Bose wave radio. Buying marginally upscale objects, I'd felt certain about my self-worth and I didn't worry. Now when family tragedy, or anything even vaguely uncomfortable, went down, I tried to remember that feeling. The night Uncle Walter died, I drove home, ignoring the plaintive screams of the world around me.

* * *

OF COURSE, WE need to look at slaves in a different way than before. The New Slavery cannot be race-based, since blacks have made far too much progress to return to unpaid servitude. I envision a system where an upper-middle-class black family can own poor white slaves, and where white yuppies can house recent Chinese immigrants in their backyard. I believe in an America heavily stratified by class, not race. I want this to be a country where everyone is free to own a slave.

The other night, I visited an ex-girlfriend of mine. Since we'd broken up three years ago, she had lived in Miami, Paris, Dublin, and Omaha, and, currently, across the hall from me. She answered the door wearing an all-purple cowgirl outfit.

"Can we have sex tonight?" I asked.

"No," she said.

I wondered whether my desire to sleep with her wasn't really a symptom of some greater longing. I tried to remember the last time I'd really cared about anything. I attempted to count from ten backward in German.

"Would you have sex with me if I had a slave?"

She looked at me, and her eyes became laser beams of desire.

"In a hot fucking second," she said.

Now, when I walk the streets of Manhattan after sundown, I carry rope and tranquilizer darts, looking for a healthy specimen. Will my slave be Central American? From Eastern Europe? What about old-school African chattel? It doesn't really matter, because the change is coming soon. The next time I find myself enmeshed in a stultifying, anxious, communal whisper at a cocktail party, I will be able to shatter the silent ice with a five-hundred-pound hammer.

"Check it out, people," I will say. "I've got a slave."

(From *A Generation on the Brink of Another Generation,* 1997)

STAND BY JOHN

I was twelve going on thirteen the spring Arizona morning when I first saw Senator John McCain. It happened a long time ago, although sometimes it doesn't seem that long to me. You hold the minutes of your life inside your heart, like a clock that never stops ticking, and then you remember everything. At least that's what John taught me, so many campaigns ago.

He came to speak at my middle school. He was confident and brave, his hair silvery even then. He was extraordinarily frank and seemingly immune from criticism, though the more conservative wing of the seventh grade tried to bring him down with difficult questions. But most of us just loved him, especially the boys, because we all dreamed of going to war, albeit with a better diet and for a shorter period of time.

In those days, I was without companionship, human or otherwise. My father had invested in a multimillion-dollar construction business, so my parents had cruelly wrenched me from the soothing arms of the New England countryside and placed me in the middle of that austere desert, away from the house servants and forest creatures who had amused me so in my earliest years.

How I needed John McCain to be my friend!

After the speech, I approached him timidly.

"Um," I said, "do you want to come over to my house tomorrow afternoon?"

He said, "Sure, you big dope."

So at 3 P.M. the next day, he picked me up from school. We ate ice cream and watched cartoons at my house. I showed him my *Star Wars* figures and he was mad because I had two Chewbaccas. That Friday, I spent the night at his place. We played Asteroids on his Atari, and later, we made POW puppets and put on a show for his wife.

As we would so often after that, John McCain and I stayed up all night and laughed. And laughed. And then we laughed some more.

THE TIMES! WHEN I was young, the wealthy suburbs of Phoenix hadn't spread like they have today, and it was still possible to creep around in the desert and scare the hell out of people. One morning, Dennis DeConcini was out trimming his bougainvillea, playing a game that he liked to call "gardener." Well, John and I left our bikes in a ditch, ran up behind Dennis, and gave him a big wedgie right through his coveralls!

That same day, we went to see *E.T.* at the mall. Afterward, over a slice, John threw his change at the guy in the pizza place. "I don't need your stinking soft money!" he said.

He had quite the temper, but God, he was a hero.

Another summer, we chucked a dozen eggs into Barry Goldwater's mailbox. Before we could run away, the old Cro-Magnon appeared at his front door with a fat-barreled shotgun. We thought we were so busted, but Barry just smiled and told us we reminded him of back when he was a kid, and also back when he was a senator. He took us inside and poured the Glenlivet.

"Extremism in the defense of liberty is no vice," he said.

"Yeah," said I, "and Joanna Stein is pretty hot, but she's in tenth grade and I don't have a chance."

I went East to college at age fourteen and soon was awash in honors and praise. John himself got pretty busy with the Keating Five trial. But at least once a year, he'd come visit me at school and crash in my dorm room. We'd stay up all night smoking and reading Rilke, and sometimes we'd take the train downtown and sneak into bars with our fake IDs. By then I had lots of friends, but when Old John from Arizona would visit, I'd drive a little faster, drink a little harder, and give passionate speeches in the student union about campaign-finance reform. I was going to drive big money out of American politics once and for all, and junior year, I was going to get my own apartment.

Now I am a journalist, and I see that my fellow members of the press love John as much as I do. Sometimes I get jealous, but John always makes me feel important. A few months before he declared, I spent a week with his family at a resort in Jamaica that allows partial nudity. One night, as we stared at the sky, partaking of that magical weed, marijuana, John offered me unlimited access to his presidential campaign.

"Come along," he said. "It'll be fun."

I was tempted. After all, it's not every day that your best boyhood chum runs for the White House. My entire career, it seemed, hinged on this opportunity. But then I realized that I shouldn't hitch onto a fading star when my own was burning so brightly.

"Sorry, John," I said. "I've had it with the small time."

I may never know what it's like at the center of a serious presidential race, but still, I have had a real buddy in my life, and how many people can make such a claim? Call me a suck-up or call me a weenie. Tell me I peddled my soul to the Republican Party. I don't care, because I'll never have another friend like John McCain.

Jesus, does anybody?

(From *Democratic Perils,* 1999)

A DOCTOR CANNOT
SAVE YOUR LIFE

The first time I saw the patient, it was the middle of my lunch hour, and I knew that he was already fated to die. To preserve his anonymity, I will call him Alan Bernstein, though his real name was Raul Hernandez.

"How are you feeling today?" I said, my mouth full of shrimp focaccia.

"I have a mild headache, and a little nausea," he said.

I leaned forward and felt his forehead. It seemed warm, but that may have been because I was wearing leather gloves. I began poking his tummy.

"Hee, hee!" he said. "That tickles!"

I realized that I had no concept of what to do next. I was merely a writer posing as a doctor in order to produce a series of important articles for several even more important magazines.

So I guessed.

"Nurse!" I shouted. "Get this man a morphine drip. STET!"

Within minutes, he was numb on a table, under full anesthesia. I had cracked open his chest. Hmm. His heart appeared to be beating, for the moment. His lungs were laboring a bit. What was that swollen blue thing near the liver? Why was his leg suddenly twitching spastically? I thought, look at all the blood!

Damn it.

I am such a bad doctor.

BUT I'VE DISCOVERED that I'm not alone. Only a decade ago, doctors in the United States were decent at their jobs. Now, it is estimated that they kill at least six hundred thousand people every year. Most of those deaths are accidental, but there's still definitely a problem. Doctors withhold critical diagnostic information, and they distribute the wrong drugs. They perform surgeries with rusty knives. Frankly, they have no knowledge of medicine at all.

The problem begins early in the education process. When I attended medical school for a few weeks last year, my professors seemed disenchanted with patient care. I was instructed to see patients as superfluous anomalies that got in the way of partying. "They are idiots," I was told, "and they're going to die eventually anyway."

On my first day of class, the professor posed this problem: "A mother is in labor. Should you give her hormones to stimulate stronger contractions? Should she have an epidural shot? Should the doctor use forceps or perform an episiotomy? What about a caesarean section?"

Several students raised their hands, but the professor disregarded them.

"I don't know," he said, "and I don't care. Screw her. Let's go have a beer."

SUPPOSE YOU'RE A doctor, like I am, at least temporarily. You are presented with a patient, a middle-aged man or woman with cancer of some sort. Your first aim is to get the patient to feel at ease. Your second, more difficult, aim is not to kill them. For instance, despite my extreme lack of experience, I am considered a cancer specialist in my hospital. Of course, I have no idea how chemotherapy functions, or how a mammogram is performed. Every time a patient comes in, I say, "Ha. Ha. Looking good. Looking good. Let's get some X rays."

Let me discuss one more case, so you understand. This patient (for the sake of privacy, a forty-five-year-old man) was a twelve-year-old girl named Belinda who had been injured during a soccer game. She was very pretty, if awkward, and exhibited potential for intelligence. I thought that maybe I could date her in a few years.

Her mother brought her hobbling into the ER. Her left eye appeared to be discolored, so I applied an ice pack.

"Does that feel better?" I asked.

"Yes," she said.

Perhaps my skills were improving.

But four days later, I entered Belinda's hospital room and found her covered in sweat and barely breathing. Her left foot had swelled to the size of a cantaloupe. Her chart indicated that she hadn't eaten in seventy-two hours. I took her blood pressure: zero. Oh, wait. That's because I'd applied the strap backward. Still, it seemed low. I wondered if the anabolic steroids I'd prescribed for her had taken effect yet. Or maybe I'd stitched her up badly after removing her appendix. Sometimes after surgery, a bacterial infection gets into the bloodstream and triggers a massive, system-wide response. As if I have any idea what that means.

Belinda's mother came into the room, weeping.

"What's happening to her?" she cried.

"There, there," I said. "She's going to live, but probably won't walk for at least a year. I did the best I could."

Unfortunately, that was true, and I felt bad. Like most Americans, this woman had no idea that our hospitals are staffed almost entirely by badly educated incompetents, and by the journalists who impersonate them. She seemed so loving, so trusting, and like her nearly dead daughter, she was cute. No husband or boyfriend had shown up at the hospital for support; so I guessed

THE NEAL POLLACK ANTHOLOGY OF AMERICAN LITERATURE

that she was single, and that she would need some soothing pretty soon. Finally, something I could provide!

I nodded sorrowfully, knowingly, and kissed her gentle lips. We were all in God's hands now.

(From The Serpent and the Scepter, 1977)

AN INTERVIEW WITH MY SISTER, WHO IS A LESBIAN

Everyone in my family is heterosexual, with the exception of my sister, Sharon, who is a lesbian. What goes on in a lesbian's head, when she is alone, or with another lesbian? Who could know the answer but another outsider, a writer like myself? When we were growing up, it was always I who felt different, interesting but lonely, excluded from the family pack. It's not easy being a National Merit Scholar at age eighteen, much less at fifteen, or even thirteen, which I was. Even then, Sharon's giving lesbian heart was open to me, so when she came out to the family a few years ago, I was especially accepting.

Sharon later said she appreciated my sensitivity, which had been attuned by my groundbreaking and remarkably entertaining literary studies of gay beaches in France, Italy, and Israel. She was also impressed that I had written a prize-winning book of short stories featuring gay and lesbian protagonists, and that I had drafted San Francisco's original domestic-partnership ordinance.

"It's almost like you're gay yourself," she said.

She is so adorable.

Last month, I interviewed Sharon before a live audience at Lincoln Center. We discussed what it means for her to be a lesbian. She was easy to talk to, totally at peace with her lesbianness, and the hundreds of my fans that turned up made her feel welcome and made no lesbian jokes during the proceedings. A partial transcript of our conversation appears below. The results were surprising and delightful.

ME

Growing up, it was always I who felt different. A stranger in a strange land, as it were. But now it turns out that you, in fact, were a lesbian the whole time.

SHARON

It's true. In junior college, my friends and I, some of whom were lesbians and some who weren't, would talk about you and your accomplishments all the time. "How is your brilliant and successful brother?" they would ask.

ME

Everyone always wants to know.

SHARON

Yeah. They said, "Have his performances in New York City been held over yet another week due to standing-room audiences?" Proudly, for months, I would reply, "Yes, and his appearance on the new David Byrne album is being praised by critics as well." As we talked about you, sometimes I would forget that I was a lesbian altogether.

ME

Did you have that problem while you were growing up?

SHARON

Not really. I didn't even think about it most of the time, because I was so busy being proud of you. After the Philadelphia Eagles drafted you, Mom, Dad, and I were so elated. We were even more thrilled after you turned down their generous salary offer to do famine-relief work in Africa. I even talked about you on my first date with a woman. How could I not? In fact, she'd heard of you. "Didn't I see your brother on *Nightline*?" she asked me over gin-and-tonics. "Yes," I said. "Three times last month."

ME

I feel bad. I should not be the measure of all human success. The bar is simply too high for most people.

SHARON

Come on . . .

ME

I get so busy that sometimes I feel disconnected from you and the family. I feel like Mom and Dad don't understand the mind-numbing lust that bubbles just slightly below my placid skin.

SHARON

No. Don't be silly. They know all about your sexcapades, and still think you're the warmest, most generous, most caring person in the world. Why, I remember when I was feeling blue one time about a lesbian-related matter, and you not only consoled me over the phone and sent me more than a hundred dollars' worth of flowers, but you also flew out and counseled me using a revolutionary psychotherapeutic technique you'd developed.

ME

And it worked?

SHARON

It gave me more confidence as a lesbian than ever. While you were directing that documentary in Bosnia, I said to my then-lover, "None of this would have been possible without my handsome, successful brother." I guess she agreed, because as soon as you returned home, you and she started dating.

ME

Yeah. Sorry about that. She made the first move and it took me totally unawares. We just had a profound sexual connection, like I do with many people.

SHARON

How could I blame her? I swear. Sometimes I just don't know how you do it. You own a loft in Brooklyn and know all these famous people. All your girlfriends are beautiful and brilliant. You've written so many novels, and traveled to Cuba, and you party with rock stars! Compared to you, I feel like nobody . . .

ME

Now, Sharon, being director of sales and accounting for Chris and Carl's Plumbing Supply and Repair doesn't make you nobody. In fact, I tell people all the time about you and how proud I am of you, my sister, the lesbian.

SHARON

Oh, you don't have to do that. I understand that you're busy. Just knowing that you're there in New York and totally successful makes me happy. Mom, Dad, Grandma, and I talk about you every night over dinner. Then, before the reruns of *M*A*S*H* come on, Mom and I pray for you. We know you meant everything you said in that *Vanity Fair* article you wrote about being an atheist, but we still believe God is on your side.

ME

I'm grateful for all your support, my lesbian sister. Without you and your people, we would all live in a simpler time, without lesbians. You are a survivor in a world where far too many people are dead. Bless you.

SHARON

No, bless you, for you are the greatest living writer.

At this point Sharon began to weep, mildly at first, but soon it turned to sobbing, and then to howling, and we were forced to leave the stage. Nothing, it seemed, could stanch her screams, not even the extra-strong sedatives I had in my jacket pocket. Poor dear. The burden of near-prominence had weighed her down, as it does so many ordinary Americans. They cannot attain the level of celebrity that I have, and shouldn't be asked to try.

Rest now, my sister the lesbian, in Bellevue, where your care is constant. When you are healed, I will still be here for you to admire. That is my solemn promise.

LAKE MINNESOTA DAYS

It's been a quiet week in Lake Minnesota. Pastor Engquist's wife, Lorna, sat in the hot dish again. This ruined Sunday supper at the church somewhat. But Bjorn Bjornsen went out on his boat, cast his rod, and soon pulled in a thousand walleye, so everyone was feeling better within a matter of hours.

The regular customers at Ingemarr Johannsen's barbershop, Roy Royquist, Lars Larquist, and Casey Caseyquist, all showed up at the exact same time for their weekly haircuts. Lake Minnesota people, as you know, are patient, and the men alternated snips, one-third of their hair at a time, until they had spent a pleasant afternoon talking about outboard motors, Lutheranism, and Daunte Culpepper's rushing statistics.

Over at the Hot Box Café, Sven Svenson was pining away for Frieda Friedricks, who, Sven figured, was the most beautiful waitress to pour Sanka there since his wife had left him so many years ago. All night, Sven Svenson looked out the window at the moon and remembered the summer afternoon when his wife Petra left for Bosnia to work as an army nurse.

I hope that Turkish soldier takes care of her, thought Sven. I hope he has a nice house for her on a lake somewhere.

"More pie, Sven?" asked Frieda.

Sven sighed and asked Frieda to marry him instead.

Frieda, as always, declined.

A bus pulled up to the terminal, and out came the junior-high handbell choir, two of whom had just had sex during a regional competition in Chicago, and Torkel Torkelson, who had been caring for his elderly mother at an expensive Jewish-owned rest home in Eau Claire. Last off the bus was John Johnsen, young writer and hopeful radio personality, returning home after ten formative years in New York City.

John Johnsen was tired of his apartment in the East Village, of sparking a joint and walking down to Tompkins Square Park to watch the police wreak abuse upon the freaks and their dogs. He was done with the cocaine and the models and all the burdens that come with being a successful writer. He had come home to Lake Minnesota, to the seedbed of his patented regional style.

He walked down Ventura Avenue, under the soft glow of the streetlamp. He saw hooligans chase the town's only black resident, who screamed in terror. He saw the old men eating their mint cookies at the bait-and-tackle store. He breathed in the moisture, the sawdust, and the gasoline. The church steeple loomed gently before him, and across the street, Edna's whorehouse and its inviting lights beckoned. He was home.

John came upon the white wood-frame house where he had grown up, where he had listened to the Green Hornet on the radio and watched his grandfather fall into a coma, a state he hadn't left for thirty-four years. The door was unlocked, as always, and, as always, John Johnsen's mother sat at the kitchen table with a bottle of bourbon, a copy of the collected writings of Martin Luther, and a steaming bowl of cranberry oatmeal.

"Hello, Mom," said John Johnsen.

"Hello, John," said Mom. "How was New York?"

"The last decade has been wonderful, Mom," John said. "I must tell you about it sometime. But first . . ."

"She's here, John," Mom said. "She's waiting for you upstairs."

There, in John's boyhood bedroom, with its posters of George Mikan, Fran Tarkenton, and Rod Carew, among his Prince albums and Replacements EPs, lying atop his now-valuable Minnesota North Stars bedspread, was Inge Svenson, in a white cotton nightdress, looking just as splendid and Nordic as the day John had left her there, ten years ago.

"I'm home, baby," John said. "Are you still a virgin?"

"Oh, yes, John," Inge said. "I, and all of Minnesota, have longed for the day when you would return and once again make us your own."

John Johnsen took off his Yankees cap, removed a lighter from his front pocket, and set aflame his New York Public Library card. He was done with the latest issue of *Vanity Fair,* and he burned that as well. He had come home to Lake Minnesota, and to his virgin bride.

Later that night, as John Johnsen smoked a Lucky Strike in the room of his youth, and Inge, utterly sated, gasped for oxygen in the bed behind him, he knew that he had made the right choice, because in this state, we wait for our literary heroes, and then we have sex with them. We're glad to see them. Now. And forever.

And that's the news from Lake Minnesota, where all the men are funny, all the women want to date me, and all the children attend well-funded public high schools.

(From *Lake Minnesota Days: A Boyhood Romance,* 1984)

TO SEARCH FOR THE
CELTIC TIGER

Polly was a slim girl of nineteen, she had light soft hair and a small full mouth. —James Joyce, *Dubliners*

On June 16, 1999, a day that I will play over in my head until the world implodes, a magnificently good-looking Venezuelan woman (and former lover of mine) named Carmela invited me to her IPO party in New York City. Many of my fellow journalists were in attendance, and they were all pleased to see me, if a little envious of my latest accomplishments. But when I arrived, Carmela was talking to a famous British Web-concept designer, and the envy was suddenly mine. As she regarded him raptly, he said,

—Three years ago, I didn't even have a fax machine in my hotel in Dublin. Now there's a laptop in every room. And it's all because of the Tiger. The Celtic Tiger has changed everything. I said,

—A Tiger? In Ireland? Really! Can you see the Tiger if you visit?

—It's everywhere, he said. The Tiger has reached the smallest village.

I was stunned. The last time I'd visited Ireland, people were destitutely merry and everything was very cheap. Also, I'd gotten drunk. But now I could see the new Ireland more clearly than I'd ever seen anything: a Celtic Tiger, with green-and-white stripes and jade eyes, roaming the valleys and crags, inspiring the Irish people to economic success. This was a great story, perhaps one of the most vital of our time! A country's rebirth had been sparked by a rare species of cat. Why hadn't anyone covered this yet?

Why, I thought, if I could find this Tiger, Carmela might even sleep with me again. I pledged to catch the next flight to the Emerald Isle.

Twenty minutes later, I was in the air.

THE MORNING SCUDS in across Dublin, an Irish-accented morning promising freedom and perhaps sausages, and I am ready to roll. The landlady of my bed-and-breakfast pours tea at the table. Stately and plump, I come from the stairhead, bearing a bowl of lather on which a mirror and a razor lie crossed. The landlady says,

—Would you please put my husband's shaving kit back in the bathroom?

The breakfast area is hung with portraits of great leaders from Irish history—Parnell, Connolly, Collins, Bono—and with a curious wallpaper that appears to be made out of stock-ticker material. My landlady serves me cereal, a hard-boiled egg, and some calamari topped with a dollop of osetra caviar. She is a sour thing, with her nose pinched too tight by a pair of spectacles. Her hair is done in an austere bun. From what I have read about the hard lives of Irish women, I feel I already know her. I say,

—I am very sorry for the molestation you suffered long ago at the hands of your uncle Pete.

She slaps me, hard, across the mouth, so I change the subject.

—Well, then, I am sorry that you ate nothing but coal as a child.

—I did not.

All is quiet, save for the whirring of a DVD player in the

other room and the far-off chopping sound of one of Dublin's brand-new public helicopters. I say,

—Landlady . . .

—My name is Rosenberg.

—I didn't know there were Jews in Dublin!

She grimaces, palpably, and says,

—Yes, there are Jews in Dublin.

—Well, then, Mrs. O'Rosenberg, what can you tell me about the Celtic Tiger? Has it bitten anybody lately?

—Bitten?

—Yes. Where is this tiger now, and does he bite?

Mrs. O'Rosenberg begins to laugh, softly at first, and then even more softly. She says,

—Thank you for a most entertaining morning. Now I have to go conduct some E-trades.

The Celtic Tiger skulks nearby. I can smell the bastard.

THE DAWN IN Donegal is verdant and harmonious, but what do I care? My eyes strain in defeat as I gaze into the leaping hills, and Carmela's luscious four-poster seems so many leagues away. My search for the Celtic Tiger has taken me to Cork and Kerry, Wicklow and Clare, and a bunch of counties of which no one has ever heard. Now, a week later, I have come to the wild country, without seeing a single paw print, or evidence of a mauling. The sun rises hot and round, and I feel a sad tenor looming in my throat. I sing:

The pale moon was rising above the green mountain
The sun was declining beneath the blue sea
When I strayed with my love to the pure crystal fountain
That stands in the beautiful vale of Tralee . . .

A man becomes visible at the door of an enchanting house that is nestled nearby. He is desiccated and old, and waving a cane. He looks exactly how one would expect an old Irish man to appear, only more so. Could he be a magical figure from Celtic myth? Wouldn't that be wonderful? I shout,

—Top of the mornin' to ya, Mr. Leprechaun!

—Tourists! he says. I am not a goddamn leprechaun!

—Sure you're not.

I wink. Perhaps my singing will persuade him to give me a pot of gold, and, as the morning dew begins to melt away from the wispy tips of azure grass, I continue:

She was lovely and fair as the rose of the summer
Yet, 'twas not her beauty alone that won me
Oh no! 'Twas the truth in her eye ever beaming
That made me love Mary, the Rose of Tralee . . .

—Would you stop that? says the old man.

—Oh. I'm sorry. Am I bothering your sheep?

—I don't have any damn sheep! I am trying to watch the NBA finals on my new satellite dish!

I sigh, scanning the countryside again for a sign, any sign, of a splendid green tiger with indelible economic powers. But Ireland is no longer delightfully rural, or even European; it's like Orange County, California, only without the beach, and with a lot more hitchhikers. There's so much technology now, and it's ruining my feature story.

THE LAST TIME I was in Galway, I drank many a pint in a comfortable pub that had portraits of pirates on the wall. I enjoyed several evenings at an out-of-the-way experimental theater, and had an ample taste of the famous Irish craic, which is a Gaelic word that means "crack."

But now I cannot even recognize the town. My favorite pub has been replaced by a café called Exploring the Gaelic Internet. The theater, once an international gathering center for bohemia, is currently featuring Frankie Avalon in a musical tribute to the actor Joseph Bologna. Meanwhile, my formerly charming B&B

has been transformed into a seventy-five-room motor inn, complete with a restaurant that serves a hideous Seafood Benedict, made with imitation crab. I am beginning to think that this Celtic Tiger is a poisonous beast.

I enter a curious establishment. The walls are done in a tasteful brownish-yellow faux finish that gives the appearance of antiquity. The only other decoration is a nude photograph of Oscar Wilde, which hangs over the bar.

After ordering a Guinness with a plate of ostrich bangers and cranberry-cilantro mash, I look around. There are no women in the entire place, which I find strange. A group of men are across from me, shouting, cheering, laughing, jesting, and having a good time; I long for my own buddies back home, who admire me so much. Remembering the lyrics to as many Pogues songs as possible, I approach these men in the spirit of friendship.

—How are yiz, ye gobshite bastards? I say.

—Excuse me?

—Nice to meet you, you maggot arseholes!

—Leave us alone, man. We're celebrating our Web site launch.

—Hah. Hah. You blokes are just a bunch of blooming eejits!

—Go away.

They all stare at me. They have stopped being joyous. Myself, I am sad, but not defeated. I'm sure they will bond with me. They are Irishmen. I speak:

—Sad to say, I must be on my way. So buy me beer and whiskey before I go and bugger your mums up the arse.

They are out of their chairs instantly. One of them seizes my arms. Another strikes my stomach. Others are kicking at my head and my groin. Then I am on the ground. My mouth is filled with blood, which spills onto my Aran sweater. Before the blackout, I think:

—Ireland, at last!

I wake in a gutter. An exquisite woman is standing over me, daubing my forehead with a moist cloth. She is from heaven, or so

I think. I am filled with an unexpected longing; I want her to walk to the store to buy the liver for my dinner. I croak,

—The Tiger . . .

—What?

—Where is the Celtic Tiger?

Her laughter drowns out the sound of pain in my ears. She says,

—It's not a real tiger. It's a nickname for an economic effect caused by the creation of high-technology jobs with the aid of foreign capital.

—Oh. Oh, God, no!

She says,

—I am from the government. We will give you five hundred pounds if you promise to leave Ireland and never return.

I think well that's not really bad money for a freelancer and then I ask her with my eyes to take me to the airport so she lifts my broken body yes and I draw her purse down to me so I can feel her breasts all perfume yes and she smacks my head and I am in agony and we drive past spacious office parks and people wearing expensive shoes and yes I said yes I will Invest.

(From *Ireland, My Ireland*, 1998)

THE RISE AND FALL OF
THE NEW ECONOMY

I am sitting in an office in a city with no name. It is 6 A.M., some months past summer, 1999, and I am making money. We are all making money these days, and not even trying to. The money is just there, and it calls to us, in low voices:

"Yoo-hoo! Can you see me? It's money!"

Making money is that easy for us, and sometimes we play Ping-Pong with whimsical paddles bearing the images of cartoon characters. When we are hungry, men in orange vests bring us ice cream and delicious rice with lemongrass curry. They never ask for tips and never stay for tea. They are making money, too. Even the wind is making money, and exercise is something that happens in the exercise room, like reading *Entertainment Weekly*.

I came to this place as a reporter. A few months ago, between novels, I looked up from my desk. The words "New Economy" were in the air outside my apartment building, literally, on a billboard that I could see from my study, and on the billboard was the picture of a female robot.

This, I thought, was a phenomenon worth investigating. I called a prominent editor friend of mine, who I'd had sex with the night before.

"There's a New Economy," I said.

"No one has ever written about it," said Tina.

"May I have permission to do so?" I asked. "In a pretentiously cute semi-ironic style?"

"Yes," she said. "You certainly may, and I will pay you seven dollars a word."

But that was not enough, even at thirty thousand words. Instead, I have joined the New Economy, because the New Economy has no rules, as I have learned. You do not have to capitalize your name. You can write articles, not about other people, but about yourself, and people will publish them, and you can still make money other ways as well. If you make money, it is the greatest story in the world, and it is yours alone.

IT IS MIDNIGHT now, and still everyone is here. We are naked, platonically, and we are giving neck rubs to one another in the conference room. One of my fellow employees, whose name is Chad but I will call him Brad, just wrote an article about himself for *Red Herring*. Another, whose name is always Emily, has a three-article contract for the same magazine I do, and also a column about herself in a weekly paper that does not admire my work. One of a thousand Brians has had his life story optioned for a movie, based on a profile he did of himself in another weekly, which used to be a glossy monthly.

"It is extraordinary," I say.

"Yes," he says, "and now I must return to my workstation, full of hope about my contributions, yet also doubting what I have become."

"That's how we all feel," says Emily. "That is why we must write about ourselves."

THEN IT IS April 2000, or May, or a subsequent month, and the New Economy is over. We watch, agonized, as our boss commits hara-kiri live on CNBC's *Market Wrap*. What will become of us, we wonder? Will we still be able to eat at diners staffed by supermodels? Will they take away our Rollerblades?

"I am a worthless husk!" shouts Brad who is really Chad.

He has just received a call from the people at *Business 2.0,* who no longer want him to write about himself for them. Emily has been reduced to writing parodies of Internet parody sites for other Internet parody sites. The air is wretched with the hideous smell of burst bubbles.

Emily approaches my desk, which is barren now of everything but floor plans for an office that will never be built.

"I have not made love to a man in nearly three years," she says.

Her magnificent breasts heave like the falling tide. I console her in my arms, and three minutes later, our lovemaking is over.

"Thank you for that gift," she says.

"De nada," say I.

ALL MY FRIENDS from the New Economy have gone now, taken their feeble remaining tens of thousands of dollars and purchased houses in Costa Rica and Thailand. Or they are in their apartments, reorganizing their files, trying to sell their memoirs. Such a sad story, really, that a generation of upper-middle-class American kids thought they could get rich without really having to work. I feel nothing but pity, and also shame. I wonder if the story will ever really be told.

The phone rings.

"Hello," I say. "It's me."

"The New Economy is dead," says my editor.

"I know," I say.

"You should write about it," she says. "The death. And how young people are sad."

"I have often wanted to," I say.

"That, and nice suburban girls becoming dominatrixes, are the leading stories of our age," she says. "I will pay you a reduced rate of six dollars a word."

I sigh. History, yet again, is a bastard, and I its midwife. The billboard outside my study has been replaced by one of a shirtless Nathan Lane. Through an open window, the city shudders in my face.

Its breath is cold, and I begin to write.

(From unpublished manuscript, 2001)

INTERLUDE:
THE POLLACK-
WILSON LETTERS

In the summer of 1950, I began a remarkable correspondence with Edmund Wilson, the Dean of American Literature, which lasted until his unfortunate death. Wilson and I had much in common. Our shared growing disdain for Stalinism led to his translation of my book, A Growing Disdain for Stalinism, *into Russian, and we watched happily as it contributed to the Great Thaw in that troubled land. We also both married the novelist Mary McCarthy, though my union lasted only two weeks and was quickly quashed by a judge in Reno. At the time our exchange of letters commenced, Wilson had already secured the publication of my criticism in* The New Republic *and* The New Yorker. *But we both had literary reputations to protect, and since literary men write letters that are collected into fat volumes after they die, we went ahead, despite our innate preference to get drunk or go to the movies instead. A few excerpts follow.*

March 26, 1951
Albergo della Citta
Via Sistina
Rome

NP:

I find it impossible to eat more than two meals a day here, not because of the quality of the comestible offerings, which is excellent, but because I cannot stop rereading your fictional treatment of the life of Hannibal. I liked it so much that I bought three copies and find myself alternating chapters among them. You are more inescapably the artist than anyone I have ever met personally, and it chills my blood. Europe, meanwhile, appears to be recovering from the ravages of war, and you should get over here and write about it before it falls prey to a lesser chronicler. Myself, I am trying to put pen to paper, but when your work looms before me like a Hydra of prose, I am cowed. I hope your testimony before HUAC is a successful one. All my love to Vera-Ellen.

Regards,
Bunny

December 6, 1956
New York City

Dearest Bunny,

Well, *Europe: The Forgotten Continent* has been published in the States, despite the efforts of the lawyers to keep it safe from our impressionable youth. Already, the moralistic firestorm has begun, and the calls for a public burning emanate from the more hayseed corners of this disturbed republic. In that vein, I reread your *Memoirs of Hecate County* last night, and, I must be honest, fell asleep around page 15. Will give it a better effort tonight. Meanwhile, I have fallen in with an intriguing group of young men from Columbia University who claim they will turn American literature on its head. This Ginsberg fellow is certainly excitable and charming, but Kerouac seems a bit of a mama's boy with a chip on his shoulder. Strangest of all is a character named Burroughs, who last night introduced me to the joys of roach powder. I fear that, for me, the demon whiskey has met his match. Tell Mary I say hello.

> Goodbye to all that,
> NP

> August 12, 1966
> Albergo Santo Cristi
> Via Cremini
> Florence

NP:

Mornings here are unbearably hot, but there's always, thank the Lord, more wine. My literary activities occupy me in the sober moments. I have finished my play about the life of Byron and am compiling my grocery lists for whatever future biographer stumbles across my unfortunate history. In the evening, the prostitutes stroll under a nearby bridge and fill my bloated frame with pathetic spasms of lust.

What of you? I hear the reaction to *Leon: A Man of the Streets* has been universal and loud and that Sidney Poitier will play your protagonist in the film version. How can you top yourself? Perhaps your upcoming trip to Saigon will provide further grist for the mill, as war always was a specialty of yours. Remember those immediate post-WWII years, when we were working on that libretto about Fascism? Sometimes as my eyesight fails me, I retain clarity by recalling your remarkable metronomic skills and facility with the ladies. God bless you and keep you in these trying and intolerant times.

> Cheers,
> Bunny

April 19, 1968
Da Nang

Bunny:

Your study of Valéry and Baudelaire gave me fortitude during a vicious firefight with Charlie, and I discovered subtle profundities in your analysis that had previously eluded me. Still, I have more earthly concerns these days, as I write to you from the ninth circle of hell. No more than that coward Nixon can extricate America from this most immoral of wars can I remove myself from Vietnam. There is truth to be told about what is going on here, and it seems to me no other American writer has the courage to do so. Now I must dash. The acid appears to be kicking in and the lights are bright and many-colored. I hope the water is cool in the family pond this summer.

Affectionately,
NP

March 10, 1971
The New Yorker
No. 25 W. 43rd St.

Dearest Nealster:

I am dying. Perhaps not today, but certainly some time this year. In the meantime, writing consumes my conscious hours. More specifically, I am writing a book about you and the friendship that we have shared, as it has been the defining relationship of my life. You have touched me like you do everyone: forever and ever. Amen.

Your life of Tocqueville is remarkable, as is your recent trilogy of short novels about Cambodia. Hopefully, you will not write anything else this year, because I am almost entirely blind, and so, so tired. In my waning hours, the memory of a lifetime of your work will give me fortitude as I prepare to ascend to that final, heavenly panel discussion in the air. Please give my love to Ms. Loren, or whoever shares your bed these days. Now, my friend, I say adieu.

Love,
Bunny

PS: Congratulations on the National Book Award. You deserved it.

INNOCENCE, BRIEFLY:
For a few short years I was not burdened by the weight of responsibility my talent would soon thrust upon me. (c. 1931)

WHEN THE WORLD WAS YOUNG: *On Jack's yacht, c. 1960.*
(Photo: Jacqueline Bouvier)

PARADISE LOST, CAMARADERIE GAINED: *Vietnam was only tolerable when on drugs. Occasionally, I would pick up a weapon and avenge my fallen buddies.*

AMONG THE LILLIPUTIANS:
Berkeley, 1972. On a panel with the lesser poets. (Photo: Mellon)

WOMEN NEED NOT APPLY:
The wilds of Africa, neither as wild or as African as reputed. To my right, wealthy gadabouts. To my left, Negro manservants.
(Photo: Peter Beard)

A NOBLE BUT FORMLESS STRUGGLE IN CHIAPAS: *Among the revolutionaries, in casual wear.*

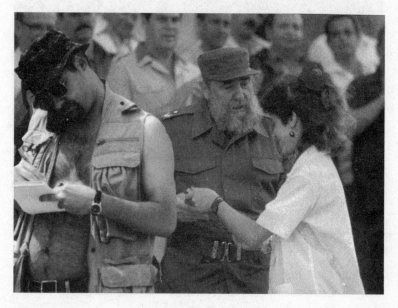

IS HE STILL TALKING? *On deadline, ignoring the patriarch in his unwilling autumn.*

AMERICA RISES. A JUST WAR FOR A NEW DAY:
Afghanistan, 2001. I emerge from the maelstrom unscathed.
God bless the U.S.A.!

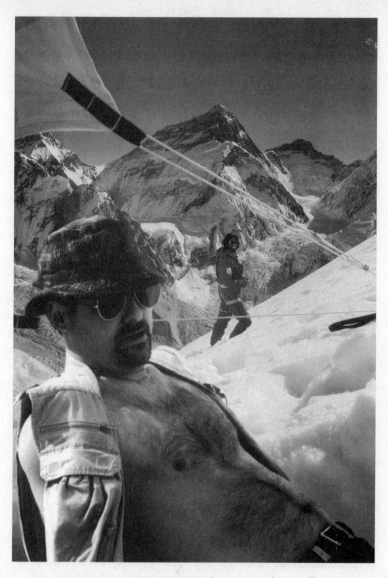

WHAT'S ALL THE FUSS ABOUT? *A respite on Mount Everest.*
No one died—that time.

WALLY:
Too young, too soft, too, too long ago.
(Photo courtesy of the author)

TEENAGERS:
THE ENEMY WITHIN

Once, youth shrouded me like a blanket, or a womb, or a cloud before the rain. Without contemplation, I climbed a forty-foot tower naked, ate a raw chicken whole, smoked a carton of cigarettes in one hour. My boyhood friend Wally Trumbull and I took my father's plane and flew to Hawaii, where we lolled through three euphonious, utopian days on the rim of a volcano, and also spent some time surfing, an experience that formed the basis for my novel The Annexation of Maui. *Those were days of jejuneness and vision, and the hot stink of unwashed underwear. Death was something that happened in Venice.*

Now I am a writer, that most wearying of professions. My ravaged glands howl desperately, echoing the voiding grief of time elapsed. So, as redemption, and on the suggestion of my editors at the New York Review of Books, *I recently undertook a project unlike any currently being attempted in American journalism. I investigated the secret world of teenagers.*

No topic receives less coverage in our media,* which is so unfair. Teenagers are the adults of the future; when we're dead, they won't be.

---

*If you haven't seen Marat Safin's ground stroke, then you're really missing something. He bends his knees into an exaggerated stance, like he's squeezing an egg between them. Keeping both hands on the racket he pulls it back, and then swings it forward. Usually he hits the ball, and often over

But because of our media's relentless bias against youth, we never see the lives of teenagers depicted. No articles have been written, no television shows produced, no movies released. Teenagers today could be utterly different than we were, or they could be amazingly similar. We don't know, because until now we haven't had the opportunity to know. This important narrative is my sober and redemptive vision that I now bequeath to you, my readers, as an immortal heritage. It brings us all, again, to the edge of youth.

The other day, I met Marcus Chen, age seventeen, at a coffeehouse in the New York neighborhood where I keep an apartment. Marcus is the founder of Youthful Americans to Save Our Cities, a multigenerational, multiethnic coalition of community organizations that proactively utilizes hip-hop lyrics to motivate inner-city residents who want to take charge of issues in their neighborhoods. At least according to the flyer he handed me.

"I was just engaged in hands-on community empowerment," he said. "A coalition of activists and I were in Kew Gardens, teaching a Salvadoran immigrant how to make Welsh rarebit. Through progressive networking, we can transform the world."

What strange child stood before me? Politics was something I dealt with at parties, on television, and, sometimes, in bed. Certainly, I had once run for Senate, a hopeless campaign that was stolen from me by those provincial ward bosses upstate, but I had never debased myself in front of a stranger before dinnertime in

---

(continued)

the net. It's really quite astonishing—when I witnessed him do this for the first time on the court at Roland Garros, I squeezed the knee of the nineteen-year-old sexual surrogate who I take to all tennis tournaments, and she emitted a little moan not unlike the ones made famous by Maria Schneider in *Last Tango in Paris,* which I co-wrote in a pique one sultry weekend at the dawn of the hedonistic age. That's when I realized that Marat Safin is a new Legionnaire, the Beau Geste of the circuit. He is a primal scream of raw metaphysical talent.

the name of activism. I had to meet the authentic Marcus Chen.

I invited him over to the house to smoke that magical weed, marijuana. He said he couldn't, because he had to fly to Seattle to protest the World Trade Organization. I can't remember exactly what I said to him, but the speech lasted a full hour, or at least fifteen minutes. Its essence was thus: You see, Marcus, life is about having a great body, eating food prepared by notable chefs, and being a successful writer with numerous sex partners. Protesting is for losers, because you're always going to lose. Nothing you do will turn out properly, and your dreams will be dashed on the sharp rocks that line the shores of the world.

By the time I finished, we were in my brownstone. Marcus's shoulders had slumped. His upper lip began to curl. Soon, it was in the full bloom of disdain.

I reached for the remote control.

"TV's fucking lame," Marcus said. "You got any video games?"

Later, as Marcus played Randy Moss NFL 2001 Super Combat Showdown: Dragon's Revenge, I burned his antigentrification flyers in my bathroom sink.

He said, "This game sucks. On Sega Dreamcast, you can totally turn Cris Carter into a flying horse."

A teenager sat in my living room, and he was bored. He smashed his head into my television screen, and yelped hideously as his forehead became a gusher of blood.

"That's my boy," I said, as I sopped his authentic forehead with a brine-soaked cloth. "That's my boy."

NEW TRIER HIGH School, in Winnetka, Illinois, boasts seven gymnasiums, a soccer stadium, and a professional-wrestling training facility. Students have a computer at every desk in every classroom, a separate lab for ten different language groups, and their own light-opera company. The average senior SAT score is 1545. Seventy-five percent of every graduating class attends Harvard, 20 percent attend Yale, 3 percent go to Northwestern, and the rest are sent to various institutions and not talked about at holidays.

In short, New Trier is just like every other high school in America. It is therefore a perfect place to investigate the American teenager. So I have come to New Trier, to talk frankly with kids about sex.

I have decided to consult an advanced-placement English class, because they are most likely to be impressed by my credentials. Perhaps, I realize, I should have told the teacher that I was coming. Still, she stops the class as soon as I introduce myself, because she has taught my novels for so many years.

"I need to be with the kids," I say, "alone."

"Of course," she says, handing me her phone number.

After she leaves, I say to the kids:

"Tell me about your sex lives, and I will publish everything you say."

I bend down to take notes, but they are silent. Some of them appear to be asleep. It's time to pull out the bazooka.

"All right," I say. "Who wants to get high?"

SEVEN STUDENTS FROM New Trier have come to Angela Shelton's house after school. Her parents are in Jakarta to attend the president of Indonesia's birthday party, so we are free to smoke marijuana and talk frankly about sex. The house is as large as an air-force base, only with more swimming pools, and I point this out to Angela.

"That's because this used to *be* an air-force base," she says.

She leans into me and lingers. I can feel her warm, soft breath on my neck.

"Then my parents bought it," she pouts, "but they always leave wittle me here all on my lonesome."

We climb a glass staircase, which is filled with butterflies, to Angela's floor. I offer the students my pipe, which I purchased from a prominent congressman of my acquaintance, but they decline. They all have their own bongs in their backpacks. Only Angela accepts.

"I like to put my lips around something long and smooth,"

she says, letting her tank top slide off her left shoulder.

Her comment has turned my insides to gelatin. But I am a writer, not a mere man, and I tell the kids that I'm amazed teenagers still smoke so much pot.

"We're stoned all the time," says Wellington, a half-Nigerian, half-Filipino son of Swedish immigrants. "Every student at New Trier is stoned every minute of every day."

Soon, I am too baked to take notes. Angela places her hand on my inner thigh and says,

"I just loooooove having sex with older men. High-school boys are so immature."

The room melts altogether away. My vision smears, and I feel wintry. All the women, all the parties, all the details of my sexual memory fade, and I imagine Angela naked, except that she is covered with rose petals. I am floating in the petals with her, rowing a boat down a Thames of rose petals, a Ganges of passion. Oh, Angela, our life on the Mississippi of roses will be so beautiful! We will light out for the territory and engage in other advanced-placement English metaphors together!

I touch her, with tenderness, and say,

"I often desire younger women."

Everyone stops smoking, stops giggling. Someone removes the O-Town album from the CD player. The kids look at me with revulsion, and a silence enters the room, like the hush in the room at Yalta just before Stalin arrived. How I remember that silence!

"Like," Angela says, "I'm totally going to call my lawyer now."

"Yes," I say. "I had better call mine as well."

Later, the Winnetka Police Department spirits me away toward my destiny of desire. I haven't been in jail since the 1968 Democratic Convention, but at least that time I deserved it. Sleep threatens to overcome my weary frame, and I cry for the innocence that I have lost.

THE ILLINOIS JUVENILE Justice Detention Center smothers three hundred acres of arid, jaundiced farmland downstate, fifty miles south of Springfield and a few meters short of hell itself. I found myself locked down there with vile teenage superpredators without morality or soul, living monsters with no redemptive merit. I was so lucky. Thanks to overcrowding in the Illinois penal system, my research continued.

One day a glimmering, robust Mexican-American of obvious merit approached me. An oversized butterfly tattoo was smeared across his chest. I had heard his name during Slipknot hour in the day room, and knew that he was respected and feared. I had seen him studying for his GED.

"I know you," I said. "They call you Mariposa."

"And they call you a dead man," he said.

"Why would anyone bother me here?" I asked. "I've written for *The Nation*."

He pointed across the yard, where a group of guys were sharpening their teeth on a jagged rock.

"Those gentlemen have been imprisoned since they were six years old," he said. "They've seen you on television and are jealous of your education."

"So?"

"They don't like writers. You're going to need protection, or else they will bite you until you die."

"And what do you get in return?"

"You will write an article about me."

"That seems fair."

"And you will help me escape from this devil-hole."

Suddenly, I saw in this Mariposa my own teenage self, except that I hadn't been Hispanic, in shape, or in jail. Mariposa! He would be out of here before his twenty-first birthday. I was garroted for Lord knows how long, but I knew that Roth and Updike would publish at least one novel apiece before my release, and I was determined not to lose ground.

"Escape?" I said. "Are you sure?"

"Yes," said he of the glittering eyes and box-office potential. "I'm stuck here in this prison, and time keeps dragging on."

"Then let us begin," I said.

And begin we did.

ARNOLD McEVOY, WARDEN of the Dixon Correctional Institute for Correctable Boys, is a flat-nosed behemoth with a boorish temper. To be summoned to his office is to risk strangulation, or perhaps flogging. He doesn't dole out discipline; he shoves it into a gaping wound. In this place, you are either a good boy or a broken boy. There is no middle ground.

One summer afternoon, as I lay on my bunk reading my 1984 novel *God and Nicaragua,* a guard rattled my bars with his baton.

"Warden wants to see you," he said.

My cellblock grew quiet. As I walked that forsaken mile, I passed Mariposa, my teenage protector. Together, we had started a prison band, the first of its kind. Our fan base on the Internet had already reached the dozens.

In his office, the warden crushed a walnut against his forehead.

"Did you distribute the following manifesto in my prison?" he asked.

He handed me a sheet of red paper bearing the likenesses of Che Guevara, Mumia Abu-Jamal, and Warren Beatty. It read:

"We all have lights out before nine o'clock here. Go to sleep in a system that continues to perpetrate ignorance amongst our spirit and amongst our minds. One that wants you not to act. Well, what if you're a night person and want to hang out? Wake up. You're part of the solution or you're part of the problem. We are sick and tired of our own complacence and going to bed early. So wake up and stop sleeping. Wake Up!

Then he said:

"I've always wanted to be in a band. The drugs, the booze, the chicks."

An instant affinity arose between the old fascist and myself. I perfectly understood his longing to participate in an essentially teenage activity. For what was I doing myself if not pretending to be a teenager for two years in jail?

"Well," I said, "I guess we could use another guy."

He said we could continue to have our band and play songs about whatever we wanted, including the one about him having anal sex with George Ryan, the governor of Illinois. But he had to be the lead singer, and he would start in the prison talent show this Friday.

As the warden plunged into a whole watermelon, face first, I was not about to argue.

RICK DE LA CERVEZA, also known as the Mariposa, was born in Los Alamos, New Mexico, the son of an atomic scientist and an anti-nuclear activist who met in a bar following an unfortunate perimeter-clearing accident. His life has been a thorough political soaking. He did solidarity work in Guatemala before he was ten, cut shop class to protest the Gulf War, refused to purchase Sting's *Dream of the Blue Turtles* album. He ended up in juvie for the most noble of reasons: lifting Henry Kissinger's wallet during the Republican National Convention.

I really didn't think he'd go for having the warden join our band. I was wrong.

"It's our pass out of here," he said. "We get him wasted after the show, and we're gone, just like that."

Because it was all-ages, we did an early show. The warden rapped our lyrics, written by the Mariposa himself. Everybody in the whole cellblock moshed and grinded to our radical message, and also beat the crap out of one another.

After, the warden personally manacled Bill, Ted, the Mariposa, and myself. He had us driven to his apartment in a prison van. Waiting there were eight women of various backgrounds, a case of tequila, and a brick of the finest Peruvian cocaine.

"All right, boys," he said. "Let's be rock stars!"

The doorbell rang.

Chicken wings!

* * *

BY DAWN, EVERYONE had collapsed into slumber, brought on by excess and orgy. I was under the influence myself, and the Mariposa had to wake me up, put my clothes on, and cut my chains with a soldering iron that he'd hidden in his underwear.

"Be free," he said.

A piggish, veined hand shot out from underneath a pile of women.

"Not a chance, Commie boy!" the warden said. He had Mariposa's ankle. But he didn't have me, and I raced for the bathroom window.

"Viva la causa!" I heard the Mariposa shout as I dove to my freedom.

As I ran, the sweat of liberty lathed my sides. I had no money and no identification. But the Mariposa had cared for me even in escape. A solid ounce of fine powder nestled in my back pocket; I merely needed to find the nearest fraternity row and I was solvent again. I felt sorrow for Mariposa, who would be in solitary for life. But at least I could tell his story, and that was freedom enough.

HITCHHIKING THROUGH IOWA, I was a scraggly, forlorn fugitive with a two-month growth of beard. Kimberly picked me up on her way to a Sandra Bernhard Fan Club convention in Des Moines.

"You have such a sweet face," she said. "You look like someone I saw once on *Meet the Press*."

"That wasn't me," I said, "and also, I didn't just escape from a juvenile prison in Illinois."

But my fortunes appeared to be transforming. Kimberly was a double major in filmmaking and gender studies. She said I would be her perfect experiment and her greatest creation.

Three days later, I was a teenage girl. My name was Paula Nealock.

I stuffed my bra with cotton, then newspaper, then some foil. The breasts looked a little crinkly, but they were fine. Kimberly's sleeveless pantsuit was exquisite on me, and I put a tampon and a photo of Freddie Prinze Jr. in my back pocket, for authenticity. Just a hint of mascara, and an extra curl to my hair, shoulder-length by now, and I was done.

"You are gorgeous," Kimberly said, "but you should probably shave your back."

THE HARDEST PART was convincing my editors in New York to bribe the warden so he'd call off the manhunt. Once that was settled, I was fine, original even. Never before has a male writer done what I am doing and felt totally secure in his sexuality.

For me, being a girl in Iowa has been easy, since it mostly seems to involve smoking cigarettes, watching television, and drinking whiskey, all of which I did when I was a man. During the day, I go to my job as a bookkeeper at the local lamb slaughterhouse, and at night, I pick up a little extra dough by waiting tables at the VFW Club.

I even have a boyfriend.

One night at the Piggly Wiggly, Walter Brenda was stacking cans of Campbell's Chunky Veal Chowder. He was a loner and a high-school dropout. He had greasy hair and bad skin. Also, he was drunk. I knew how he felt, without the high-school drop out part.

Every teenage girl remembers her first kiss, and I wanted to empathize with the feeling for an article I was doing for *Mirabella.* So Walt took me to the minigolf, and I let him kiss me. It wasn't that bad, since we were both hopped up on bourbon and amphetamines. On that mixture, I would have kissed a horse, with tongue.

A group of guys in letterman jackets were hanging around the seventeenth hole, because they liked to look at the mermaid's breasts. They saw us, and fractured the mood.

"Hey Walt!" one of them shouted. "Who's the skank?"

Walt was small, and gaunt, and defeated by years of abuse from these lummoxes. But I wasn't. No one talked to my boyfriend that way. Besides, I wasn't ugly! I was a fine-looking girl, if you ask me! I was more attractive than any of their cheer-leader girlfriends and I could write better than they could, too.

BACK IN MY apartment, Kimberly mopped my face with a rag. Walt lay on the bed, moaning something about his ribs.

"I love you, Paula," he said to me.

Kimberly looked at me sternly.

"Goddamn it," she said. "Tell him the truth."

I did. I told him everything because he was my boyfriend, even the part about how famous and successful I really was, not leaving out any details of how my father finally destroyed William Randolph Hearst. But instead of running away in out-rage, instead of castigating me, Walt laughed, cried, laughed again, cried again, and hugged me ever tighter.

"I've got something to tell you, too," he said.

He pulled up his shirt to reveal a pair of small but well-formed breasts.

"I'm really a girl," he said. "My name is Brenda Walters. And there are so many more like me."

IN THE MORNING, I take archery practice along with these fourteen-year-old boys in skirts and fifteen-year-old girls in denim. As targets, we use cutouts of football players and cheerleaders, or sometimes photos of *The Breakfast Club.* After lunch, we all meet in small groups for workshops in voguing and self-esteem, and sometimes we read aloud from the diaries of Quentin Crisp. After a brief round of hormone supplements (which I only pretend to ingest), we listen to lectures from our counselors, who tell us that the White House is out to destroy us with black helicopters and endless heterosexist press conferences. At night, we deconstruct and we burn. Tonight we set aflame an effigy of Sarah Michelle Gellar; tomorrow, I pray, it will not be Leo.

After lights out, I lie awake, afraid that someone will discover that I am not a teenager. The boy in the bunk next to me is a girl. The girl in the bunk next to her, or him, is a boy. Or perhaps the roles were reversed over the last few days; I do not know, for I have lost all capacity to discern gender. Who would have conceived, when I began this voyage into the fractured heart of American adolescence, so many days, so many articles, ago, that I would end up here, just outside of Cri de Coeur, Idaho, in a heavily fortified forest compound? But yet that is my fate. I have penetrated the secret headquarters of Transgendered Nation, an armed teenage resistance group dedicated to the overthrow of the United States government.

Walter Brenda—Brenda Walters—my boyfriend—my girlfriend—provided my entrée into this organization, which, despite the immense threat it poses to our national security, has gone completely ignored by the mainstream media. Even now, I am begging my editors to believe that this place exists, and they refuse. Certainly it sounds preposterous, and perhaps it is, but I have smelt the piney woods and felt the animals underfoot. I have witnessed the girls kick the boys' collective ass in football, and seen the boys take an hour to get ready in the morning.

They have descended, these youthful pre-ops, by the hundreds. They are angry. And they are ready for battle.

"THE LEADER IS coming," Walt says one morning.

"The Leader?" ask I.

"Yes. The one who wrote *The Turned-Around Diaries*."

We have read aloud from this book every day since I arrived at the camp. Its plot is somewhat confusing, foretelling a "great uprising" of transgendered teens in high schools around the country, a nationwide bloodbath that will stun the government into making "the author of this book" into an "all-powerful dictator who also controls the NFL." I think the book is nonsense, of course, but these youths live by it. They are lost, angry, and, judging by the grammar in *The Turned-Around Diaries*, unconcerned about proper editing techniques. I shiver in memory, as I'm reminded of Jonestown, which I escaped two days before the fall and subsequently wrote about in *Jonestown Memories: The Brink of Madness.*

Precisely at midnight, Walter and I and all the others head for a clearing, where two giant loudspeakers are playing k.d. lang's "Constant Craving" in a continual loop. Suddenly, two red floodlights slam on, and in front of a stage, two banners unfurl, one bearing the image of RuPaul and the other a likeness of Joan Crawford from *Johnny Guitar.*

The music grows louder. The night shivers with our howls. Then, at the peak of our frenzy, the Leader appears.

He is small, and old, and withered. Or should I say she? Regardless, the Leader stands before us in a green hooded cloak, which bathes his or her face in darkness. Walter is rapt beside me. I run behind a tree and turn on my tape recorder. The Leader says:

"My children. We are at a turning point in human history. A point of revenge. Of TRANSGENDERED REVENGE!"

Ten thousand teens sway and cheer.

"Of course," the Leader says, "I do not officially advocate violence, and if you kill someone in your righteous anger, and then tell them about me, OUR MOVEMENT WOULD BE FINISHED, AND I WOULD HATE YOU!"

The teens sob and rend their Dame Edna T-shirts.

"The time has arrived," says the Leader. "I want you to go to the storehouse, and take as many weapons as you need. Then I want you to return to your high schools. Do not forget your anger. You must do what you have to do, as long as I'm not implicated."

From the crowd, a sixteen-year-old shout arises.

"Kill!" it shouts.

"Of course I didn't hear that," the Leader says, "but I admire your enthusiasm."

"Kill! Kill! Kill!"

All night, the Leader cajoles, prods, and even teaches the triangle offense. Someone dressed like Dennis Rodman dances with someone dressed like Boy George. Then, most terrifyingly, a group of teen players act out the Greta Garbo cross-dressing scenes from *Queen Christina.*

Should I stop this holocaust from occurring? Or should I weave my findings into a coherent narrative? God. What a choice.

I still have not decided at dawn, when the pickup trucks arrive. The Leader's minions hand out shotguns, and we rumble off to our violent destiny.

ONE RECENT NIGHT, I desperately sought to prevent a cult of brainwashed transgendered youth from committing a nationwide high-school massacre. I felt old; I had lost my writerly abilities and nothing could make me youthful again. But then, in the parking lot of a White Hen Pantry, someone in a hooded sweatshirt slipped me the five-dollar solution along with an invitation to a party.

My prayers were answered in the form of a tasty treat, colored pink, with a little Cupid symbol embossed onto its surface. The pill tasted fresh, and the lights at the party were phat, and I danced all night long. When I got home, full of dash, I posted an emergency E-mail to the Troubled Transgendered Teens list server.

Death was off, I said. Everyone was equal under the groove. And the kids, they listened, because they sought what I sought. Sweet release was theirs, and mine.

It was time to rave.

The next three days were frenzy. Quickly, I secured a former beet-processing plant in Camden, New Jersey, and kicked out the dozens of Laotian immigrants who were living there. A few calls to friends of mine at *Interview*, and I had booked the best DJs in the world. These included DJ Skoli Skol from the Stockholm scene, Johnny Oi! from Canberra, and Macro Dreadlock Rastafari Thunderman, of course, from Warsaw. I scored a bunch of clovers, 2000 Rolls, Mickey Mice, as well as quantities of E and acid-dot supermen. It was a wicked roll and I was psyched and I came down with a lot of mellow energy.

Seven thousand kids showed for my Techno Love Parade, happy and horny. They received glowsticks, red and blue inflatable bubbles. I gave them copies of *Green Eggs and Ham*. It only cost forty dollars.

This was my Summation Rave, when the story fit together. Everyone came. Angela Shelton, who had forgiven me for my sexual indiscretion against her, flew from Chicago. The Mariposa escaped from prison at last, and now was headed to Philly to bust Mumia loose as well. Walter Brenda—Brenda Walters—brought the newly groovy transgendered army. One by one, and sometimes two by two, they hugged me. We were filthy ravers and we couldn't care less. Our shoes smelled like the old vegetables that this space once housed. The laser lights admonished the smoke like alien beacons, but we were dancing too hard to notice.

NOW, WITH EVERYONE gone, I write what I remember of them, tabulate the receipts, and know that I am the sun, or two suns, and the galaxy circulates around me. The kids will have memories and soiled clothes and perhaps unusual side effects from the Blue Popeyes I slipped them at dawn. I have a book contract, and I will care about them so much.

In a few years, America will have more teens than ever before, and they have so much money. All teenagers do is spend and work, and spend. The fools don't remember the simple joys of a lazy summer afternoon and mooching off your parents. But we are smarter adult people. Aren't we? We know how to get our slice. All you have to do is grab some cheap real estate, put up flashy lights, and pump the kids full of drugs. It will be a wild scene and you will heal the world.

The night of my Summation Rave, the hookups began at 4 A.M. Angela was getting it on with Marcus Chen, age seventeen. The Mariposa found a pile of the transgendered that he liked, and was certainly glad to be out of prison. I kissed Brenda, and Brenda kissed everyone else, and we all fell into a naked heap on the floor, covered in chocolate.

"My subjects, oh my subjects!" I shouted. "In my way, I have loved you all!"

(From *Fragments Without Forgetting*, 2000)

INTERLUDE:
THE PARIS REVIEW
INTERVIEW

June 27, 1976

Neal Pollack grants few interviews, certainly far fewer than he conducts. This conversation took place on the eve of America's Bicentennial celebration, which Pollack was to spend in Scotland, in continued protest of his country's misguided venture in Vietnam. "I know the war has ended, but I just can't get over it," he said, wiping his eyes with a gilded napkin. "The screams of my buddies still echo in my head, and then there is the matter of America's lost innocence to consider." He was putting the finishing touches on The Serpent and the Scepter, *his searing indictment of Western medicine, and had just published his first collection of poetry,* Sad Bells of the Adriatic, *which was to win the Whitbury-Pullman Prize. We sat on the balcony of his family's castle as a cool fog breathed in across a moor, and then a heath, and then a hill. His rippling musculature could not mask the sexually charged intelligence that shot from his beautiful eyes. So we began:*

INTERVIEWER

Where did you get the idea for your new book?

POLLACK

All my inspiration is derived from a solitary source: a waking, eternal longing to once again hold Wally Trumbull, my former roommate at Exeter, in my tanned and muscular arms. I remember the first night we lay together, the moonlight reflecting off his Captain America pajama bottoms, his hairless chest glistening with the tender sweat of youth. Time cannot diminish my memories of his primordial beauty and Precambrian intelligence. Later, it was 1947 in Manila. I watched agape as Wally was stabbed during a wharfside game of Pai Gow poker. Wally's insides gushed against my expensive shirt and he said, "You have to write, for me, forever."

INTERVIEWER

And write you did.

POLLACK

Oh yes. I subsequently chronicled the situation in my book *The Brutal, Racist Murder of Wally Trumbull,* which is still held up as the progenitor of today's best literary journalism. Dear God, I miss Wally so! He had such magnificent feet, like a faun's!

INTERVIEWER

I realize that this is like asking an orchard-keeper to pick the sweetest apple off the most verdant tree, but do you have a favorite work of yours?

POLLACK

Does one ask Shakespeare which he prefers: *Hamlet* or *Lear*? Or force O'Neill to choose between *A Moon for the Misbegotten* and

Long Day's Journey into Night? Would you dare ask Leon Uris to pick *Trinity* over *QBVIII?* Not bloody likely. That said, I think I like *Europe: The Forgotten Continent* best. The years I spent with the people of those unfairly disregarded countries were possibly my most memorable. I pray that the people of Provence and Tuscany will someday enjoy the prosperity they so deserve. May God give them the strength to triumph over their corrupt and decadent governments.

INTERVIEWER

Have you ever had difficulty writing?

POLLACK

It was hard for me to describe my feelings at winning my screenwriting Oscar. Hollywood is drastically over-covered as a topic and I didn't want to betray my friends, particularly Clark Gable and Carole Lombard, who were so generous to me back in my hungry days. Besides, what could I possibly add to our knowledge of the film industry? I bravely found the words, in my book *The Silver Lights of Babylon,* recipient of the American Book Award, 1964.

INTERVIEWER

As a writer, what is your greatest strength? Weakness?

POLLACK

My strengths are numerous, and include my singular felicity with language. I also bring to the table a sweeping intelligence that can sketch individually memorable characters against a vivid backdrop of history while still deploying an ironic, all-knowing narrative structure that refuses to sacrifice emotional generosity.

INTERVIEWER

But we all know that . . .

POLLACK

As for flaws, my writing is often so damn good that I have a hard time following my own act. Nevertheless, I usually succeed.

INTERVIEWER

When and where do you write?

POLLACK

Wherever and whenever I can. For instance, when I was teaching at the University of Chicago in the sixties, I would go to various blues bars on the South Side to work on a poem or perhaps an essay for *Ramparts*. One day, I looked up, and I understood that black people, or Negroes (as we called them in days less haunted by the language police), surrounded me. Suddenly, I realized that they and I shared an essential humanity, if not education level, and I felt compelled to record their experiences.

INTERVIEWER

That was an important moment for you, yes?

POLLACK

Certainly. From there, I wrote at Baptist churches, and diners, and they began to consider me one of their own. Sex followed naturally, as did membership in both the NAACP and the Black Panthers. For a brief time, I was a guest artist at the Apollo, where I opened for the soul preacher Solomon Burke. And so was born my novel *Leon: A Man of the Streets,* which Ralph Ellison always said was the book he would have written if his house hadn't burned down.

INTERVIEWER

This may be uncomfortable to discuss, but could you talk about how your friend J. D. Salinger influenced you and why your relationship with him deteriorated over the years?

POLLACK

If I must. Salinger, as you know, was once a great writer like myself. In fact, many considered him the finest writer of his generation. He had won as many awards as I have, and was on his way to more. But then something in him snapped. He began sending cryptic messages to his friends and colleagues. He would disappear for months at a time, and it was soon clear that he had gone over to the other side. One day my publishers called me into a private meeting and told me that he had gone too far. I needed to find him and terminate him with extreme prejudice. So I undertook a well-chronicled journey into the obscure heart of mankind. Strangely, I began to empathize with Salinger and his iconoclastic ways. This publishing business was madness, and I was becoming more like him as my voyage spun desperately away from me. I had to destroy him, and in the process, destroy myself.

INTERVIEWER

What is the best advice about writing anyone ever gave you and who gave it?

POLLACK

When I was a boy of twelve, Papa Hemingway sat me on his meaty haunch and said, "Fella, you are going to overtake me faster than a Jeep on an elephant hunt." When I saw him ten years later, he was sleeping off a drunk and I didn't want to bother him, but I wanted to say thank you, because he had been perfectly correct. Then there was the time that Burroughs accidentally mixed one of my manuscripts into a batch of wacky brownies, but that was Burroughs for you.

INTERVIEWER

If you weren't a writer, what would you do?

POLLACK

I'm sorry. I didn't hear the question.

INTERVIEWER

If you weren't a writer . . .

POLLACK

I was just remembering a rugby match that Wally Trumbull participated in, when we were sylvan youths at school. He soared in the air like an eagle in the movies, his tendons flexing in the placid Massachusetts wind. The wall of male flesh that comprised the other team melted away in a blur of mud and random color and Wally plunged into the end zone, resplendent, victorious, and aggressive. My heart leapt from my chest into my throat, and I didn't bother to swallow it again, because Wally had scored. He had scored for me.

INTERVIEWER

Which is the best city or town in which to give a reading? Which is the worst?

POLLACK

Once I was run out of Istanbul, but that had less to do with my reading than with my early championing of Turkish women's suffrage. I haven't since returned but trust that conditions have improved. As for the best city, I retain a soft spot for my native

Boston, though I haven't visited since 1975, but nothing beats a weekend in L.A. for cocaine and hookers.

INTERVIEWER

What is the best book you read this year?

POLLACK

There was a time, now long passed, when literature mattered in America, and it was possible for an author of quality to make a reasonable living. These days, serious writing is less an avocation and more a hobby, like polo, or chess, or sex with animals. Nevertheless, this year I did discover an excellent young author named John Jakes. He has written a subtle, beautiful book of history called *The Bastard* that I recommend to anyone.

INTERVIEWER

Who's the best book reviewer in the country?

POLLACK

I haven't read a book review written by anyone besides me in almost twenty years. Why would I?

INTERVIEWER

We look upon your writing as a quest, but for what we are not sure. Can you describe your mission as a writer?

POLLACK

My goals are twofold: one, to transform the English language. I began as a mere journeyman, but my art grows subtler as I age, and I feel myself sinking more and more deeply into the curse of genius. Second, I want to be the preeminent living chronicler of the human condition, both through fiction and nonfiction. I've got to say that I'm almost there. I regret no book that I have written, and will regret none in the future, for my work is a distillation of my time on earth.

INTERVIEWER

Shall we finish this bottle of bourbon?

POLLACK

Please. And let me make a final point. I want to make clear something few people know about me: I long to make people laugh. For too many years, my work has been burdened by seriousness and an excessive need to shake a sense of morality into America, that most immoral of lands. Now, though, with Watergate and the excesses of the sixties behind us, I am ready for humor, that highest and most subtle of art forms, and I intend to pen at least a trilogy of comic novels.

INTERVIEWER

Honestly?

POLLACK

Yes. Join me and together we will scream with joy.

INTERVIEWER

I am ready to scream right now.

POLLACK

Oh but we have barely begun, my lovely creature.

(Interview by Joyce Carol Oates)

THE COITUS CHRONICLES:
A TRILOGY IN THREE ACTS

Upon returning from a recent vacation to East Timor, I found four messages on my answering machine. One was from my stockbroker, assuring me that my shares in Halliburton were secure, and soaring. Two were from the insatiable Angelina Jolie, but she could wait a few minutes. The fourth was from an editor, who said that it was time for me to write again about sex. Since the 1975 publication of *The Hairy Animal,* I've been considered somewhat of a national expert on the topic, and I certainly have it enough. So a few days later, corporate voucher in hand, I began my journey. It took me from America to Europe and back to America again. I searched my soul and found nothing of interest. But I sure got laid. The report follows.

I. A REPORT ON THE HABITS OF THE
SEXUALLY RAVENOUS SINGLE WOMEN OF
NEW YORK WHO ALSO HAVE JOBS

In America today, some women are married, and some are not. A few weeks ago, I was reading my favorite German newsweekly, *Die Humberschlingel,* which revealed that fewer women are married today than were once married. This has created a fascinating new class of people in this country: single women. The Germans, who

THE NEAL POLLACK ANTHOLOGY OF AMERICAN LITERATURE

are very intelligent, discovered that of the thirty-seven million single American women, some of them live in Chicago, others in northern California, and others in other places. But I was shocked to discover that nearly five million single women live in New York City alone, three million of them in Manhattan. The place is just seething with single women.

"Isn't that an interesting phenomenon?" I asked my wife.

"Not really," she said.

"Oh, yes it is," I said.

As a journalist, which is my profession, I was determined to attempt what no journalist had yet attempted. A single, nearly magnetic force was drawing me to the great untold story of our age. I was going to write about the single women of New York City, and no one, especially not my wife, was going to stop me.

My initial attempts at research were rebuffed. I ventured into the nether region around Fourteenth Street and Eleventh Avenue, which had once been called the Tenderiron district, because of the tender irons that its inhabitants would apply to the bodies of interlopers. But now, this once-seedy area of wharfside bars and hurdy-gurdy houses has been transformed, by the magic of the New Economy, into a pungent flowerbed of loft offices and trendy bars.

I ventured into Pomme, a nightclub that *Time Out* has called "one of the hottest spots for sexually ravenous single women in New York." From my excellent store of foreign vocabulary, I concluded that "pomme" was French for "disco."

At the bar were a dozen women, all employed in media, high technology, or law. I could tell this because, in the manner of the new New York, they wore placards around their necks.

I approached one woman, whose sign read, "I work for VH-1. In promotions."

"Why are you single?" I asked. "Is it because you want to have sex with many men?"

Her friends surrounded me, as though they were a coven. None of them spoke, save one, who was wearing a fetching little turquoise sailor's suit. "I work for Burston-Marsteller," her sign read.

"We will eat you for lunch if you do not leave this bar at once," she said. "A new day has dawned in New York City, with a new ruling class. Ask us no questions, for we are single women, and we have power."

What a single woman she was!

I RETURNED TO my hotel, gazed at the sleeping form of my wife, and sighed. Why couldn't she be single, too?

I didn't understand the true power of Today's Single New York Woman until I recently gave a reading at Galapagos, a workingman's bar located in a hardscrabble Brooklyn neighborhood. As usual, my performance drew much laughter and awed, gaping stares. However, unlike in other cities where an hour after the show, I am left sitting alone at a table with a big wad of cash, in New York people stayed, and most of those people were women.

As drinks were bought and then consumed, the crowd began to thin slightly. Then four women formed a phalanx and headed toward me. They introduced themselves, not by name, but as a gossip columnist, an architect, a single mom with a trust fund, and a writer of cookbooks in Braille. The architect grabbed my hands, and pinned them to the table.

"You're coming with us, author-boy," she said.

A few minutes later, I found myself in the back of a limousine, and the women were force-feeding me Scotch from a funnel. The columnist tore at my belt with her teeth, and the single mom ripped off my Zegna suit jacket. The cookbook writer donned a pair of heels. Grinning lustfully, she pressed them against my chest.

"Please don't hurt me," I whimpered.

"Oh no," she said. "We are definitely going to hurt you. We are single women, and we hurt people."

By midnight, I was a heaving wreck of a man. Every part of

my body had been licked, sucked, poked, stabbed, and spilled upon. The women had penetrated all the major orifices, and a few of the minor ones as well. They smoked cigars while I gasped and bled, now dressed only in stained boxers and a torn T-shirt.

"Can you take me to my hotel now?" I asked.

"I don't think so, buddy," said one of them.

They bade the driver to stop the car, opened the back door, and kicked me in the rear.

"You have satisfied us sufficiently," the columnist said. "And now we are through with you."

Then I was on the street, at the corner of 125th and Amsterdam, and they were driving away, with a song blaring from the trunk speakers: *"Sisters,"* the lyrics went, *"are doin' it for themsehelves."*

I was glad that they were gone, and to have escaped with my life and with a narrative. I sat on the curb, wept, and wondered how I was going to get home.

Another limo pulled up. The window rolled down. Inside, I could see five women, all snorting cocaine, dressed in nothing but pink leather.

"Three of us are lawyers for the United Nations," one of them said, "The other two are librarians at Columbia University. We are on the prowl for man-flesh!"

Before I could stop them—and I couldn't really stop them— they had me hogtied and lying across their collective lap. Although I was severely dehydrated, I submitted to my fate, because in today's New York City, you do what single women tell you to.

"Good ladies of New York," I moaned against my will, "I belong to you!"

II. THE DARK GODDESS OF RUSSIA IS HORNY

During the Stalinist purges, I would stroll the Nevsky Prospekt in the snow and ponder my good fortune. Indeed, here I was, the only Western correspondent in the Soviet Union, and as the deaths mounted, my disillusionment mushroomed. I wrote to my foolish leftist friends in the United States that our Communist Barn Dances, our People's Theater performances of the collected works of Bakunin, had been terribly misguided, and my letters were quickly collected and published, to great influence. Lady Fate had once again beamed upon my literary gifts and me.

The years advanced, and I often returned to Mother Russia, both on vacation and for work. My skepticism about Khrushchev turned into a hatred for Breshnev. I was the first American journalist to take Gorbachev out to brunch, and my subsequent children's book, *A Brunch with Gorbachev,* was awarded the Caldecott Medal. I attended every SALT summit. When Chernobyl blew, I was there to provide narrative perspective. From my unique perch, I watched the Soviet Union fall, and then I drove around Eastern Europe and watched everything else fall as well. I was a witness to history, and I got a lot of mileage out of that on the lecture circuit.

But no matter how Russia, which my friend, translator, and dominatrix Masha calls "that stubborn mule of a land," has bungled its destiny, it has always endured. Now, however, I smell a threat. For I am in Russia again, and something is wrong here. I have never covered a story so full of historical portent. This is small potatoes compared to Yeltsin climbing on that tank or the mob taking over the economy. Steel yourselves for what you are about to read.

American men are coming to Russia, to look for wives.

LAST YEAR, WITHOUT warning other than several articles in the papers and an hour-long national television special, the market for Russian women blew wide open. Suddenly, wife-meeting clubs began to open up in nearly every neighborhood. The less discriminating could just go to Red Square where entrepreneurs, mostly displaced Georgians, had set up booths at which they could hawk their teenage daughters. To prove his commitment to this new economic force, President Putin sold his niece to a computer programmer from Bern for two thousand dollars. And when word reached the States, things really went nuts. Never ones to turn down cheap and easy sex, our citizens began to book their flights.

A few weeks ago, I arranged to spend the day with several clients of Blow Me, Olga, an American organization founded to match single men up with available Russian women. When I asked the group's president, a slovenly, bespectacled scientist named Peter Parker, why Russian women are so appealing, he said,

"Because they are hot sluts who don't care if you bitch-slap them around. American women are all feminists who want to talk to you about what they did at work that day. I just want a chick who'll raise my kids and suck hot gravy out of my ass if I tell her to."

"I see," I replied.

My experience in Russia had been different, I reflected. Sure, the hot gravy part was true, but I found the women of the former Soviet Union, like most of the world's women, to be fascinating creatures of mystery, especially if they liked my books. By contrast, these men from Blow Me, Olga seemed so primitive and naive in their desires.

I decided to concentrate on one man's experience for my story, since only through describing the experiences of an individual in a broad social context can a magazine reporter spin a saleable narrative for a quality publication. I chose Alan, who owned a small chain of swimming-pool stores in Indiana. He had been thrice divorced, each time, he said, from a "castrating Democrat" who wanted to "get a job" and "think for herself." He said he wanted something different.

"Just give me a woman who knows how to cook, and I'll be happy," he said, "as long as she has tits like a porn star."

We went to Kamchakta Nights, a wife-buying club near the Hermitage, in Saint Petersburg. Inside, while the music of Bryan Adams played over the stereo system, seventy-five women waited anxiously for potential husbands. They sat with their legs crossed, in demure outfits, eager for conversation.

Alan approached one, who introduced herself as an accountant named Nadia. She was twenty-seven, she said, and liked "cowboys."

"You wanna sit on my face?" Alan asked.

She slapped him hard, across the mouth, and then she slapped me, too.

"Skank," Alan said.

The process was repeated with seven other women. Sometimes Alan would ask them to "ride" his "pole" or "hork" his "rod," but the results were always the same. I got tired of getting slapped. I realized that I had to show Alan how this was done.

"These douchebags are just like the chicks back home," he said.

"Patience," I said.

In a corner sat a lovely young woman, who introduced herself as Natalya. She was a home-care nurse, she said, and was a great admirer of the Australian rock band INXS.

"Hello," I said. "I wrote *Leon: A Man of the Streets.*"

"Then I will marry you," she replied, "as that book taught what it means to be a woman."

Her arms flew about my neck and she kissed me, with tongue.

"No, no," I said, "I am not in the market."

Alan, who had been sulking behind me, came into the light.

"But," I said, "I would like to introduce you to my friend Michael Chabon."

"The author of *The Mysteries of Pittsburgh?*" she said.

Alan's eyes showed a faint glint of intelligence. "Um," he said, "sure. Would you give me a blow job now?"

"It would be an honor," she said, in broken English. "I have always wanted to suck off the man who wrote *Wonder Boys,* not to mention the Pulitzer Prize–winning *The Amazing Adventures of Kavalier and Clay.*"

Soon, the other men in Alan's group caught on to his secret method, and they were going about the room, pretending to be male American authors. The Nicholson Baker impersonator got into a wild three-way with a couple of dental technicians. James Ellroy's doppelganger was cornholed with the biggest vibrator I'd ever seen in Russia. Even the poor shmoe who, against my advice, claimed to be Truman Capote got a little tail. And I, of course, satisfied many a restless Russian book whore.

Later, as I rubbed salve onto my chapped thighs, I thought about myself, but also Russia. It is entering a new epoch of its history, one in which its women are for sale to the highest bidder. Is that really as bad as decades of Communist oppression? I asked the twins in bed with me what they thought.

"We are fine," they said in unison, "as long as we have an American novelist who wants us to satisfy his every sexual whim."

History, it seemed to me at that moment, was fortunate indeed.

III. OH, HARSH LAND OF PORN!

Recently, I felt a vague stirring in my loins, but it was not a sexual stirring. Those are common enough and easily slaked. No, this stirring was a journalistic one, and I realized that my story radar had again been activated. The stirring became a notion, and then an idea. An hour later, I had done some research, and I was stunned to discover that my stirring had been correct; more Americans are watching, consuming, and enjoying pornography now than ever before. Indeed, the Web site pornstats.com indicated that our citizens now spend nearly seventy-five billion dollars a week on dirty movies and assorted accoutrements. Shocking! How could this be possible? I asked myself. What had happened to our once vaguely innocent land?

In more puissant days, before television appearances and end-less cocktail parties began to consume my social hours, I indulged in the blacker hobbies. Stag films were common at Yale, which I attended, and at Princeton, which I also attended, simultaneously. And what healthy young upper-class scion was ever denied a three-day squat with a high-class New Orleans hooker? Even those of us with mild homosexual tendencies enjoyed our indoctrinations, and the resulting shots of penicillin. But these were pleasures for the rich, and, in less sanguine conditions, for the poor. The vast moronic middle had sex once a year, we were taught, and that sex was only for reproductive purposes, and it was usually bad.

As a lifelong creator and consumer of culture both high and low (some would even call me a culture junkie), I was naturally interested in this phenomenon, this porn-mania, as it were. However, unlike other writers—all of whom are less talented and accomplished than I, and certainly less respected—I had no interest in ogling porn stars or hanging out with them at home. I had no interest in wearing a hat that bore the words "Porn Star." I just wanted to know how, and why, porn was so popular, without indulging in prurience or cheap jokes.

So I bought a plane ticket to Los Angeles, where I had an appointment to meet with the director of *Your Ass Lick Park III: Revenge of the Clitosaur.*

"I WAKE UP horny, and I can come seventy-five times a day."

I was on a velvet divan in a shabby soundstage in Yorba Linda. My interview subject was a nineteen-year-old college sophomore named Carol, but her porn-star name was Helen Cunt.

"That's very interesting," I said. "Do you have any insight as to why the American public is watching more and more porn?"

"Wanna see what I can do?" she asked.

"Sure," I said.

She began licking her own breast.

"Ohhh, this makes me feel so good," she said. "I really want to suck you off right now."

This archaic sex talk was about what I'd expected, and I didn't need to hear more. After all, I was married, and I also had a girlfriend. In the sex department, I did not lack. So instead of submitting to the request, I asked her: "Do you think the increased presence of the Internet has made it easier for porn manufacturers to market themselves?"

"Yesssss!" she moaned. "Ohhh, baby, yesss."

I wrote her answer down. She removed her panties, and began to squirm.

"Ohhhhh!" she said. "Journalism makes me sooooo hot!"

Well, shit, I thought. Even though I may be in the running for a National Magazine Award here, I am just a man. Extreme circumstances often lead to sudden changes of perspective.

I finished my notes, and promptly came on her face.

IN THE COURSE of my research, I found out that adult-entertainment companies are at the forefront of interactive television, interactive Internet, and interactive DVD technologies. I learned the legal ins and outs of various state obscenity laws and spoke with dozens of experts. I also learned three new things to do with my testicles, and I must have come 150 times, my new one-week record.

After all my wilding, I decided to interview one of the many women who has taken production of porn into her own hands. In Portland, Oregon, I visited the offices of SMC Technologies, run by a forty-two-year-old former porn star named Lisa Craig, an attractive, confident woman who has done many things since she retired from the industry twelve years ago. She has been a construction worker, a professional chef, a hockey player, and a ship's captain. For a time in the early nineties, she was an options trader, and later joined the circus, she says, in a "public-relations capacity." Three years ago, she was working as a $250,000-a-year systems manager for Microsoft, and realized that what she really wanted to do was make porn.

"Porn degrades and humiliates women," she said, with surprising frankness. "I mean, it's all so *boring* and *stupid*. We strike the same poses and are supposed to look excited when some old guy dressed as a postman leaks a little cum onto our bellies. I want to make movies that are erotic, that turn women on."

She picked up a banana from her desk and began sucking on the tip.

"I think I know what I want . . . right . . . now," she said.

REPEATEDLY, IN MY reporting, I was asked by porn producers to star in a movie myself. They said I wouldn't know what the industry was like unless I participated in it. Still, I was reluctant, because my real story was about distributing and disseminating the product. But Lisa Craig persuaded me that with this particular story, participatory journalism was the only way to go. That afternoon, after a quick three-way with her secretary, we banged out a script.

My character was to be named Ernest Hemingcock, and he was the Greatest Living American Writer. He would travel to Sweden to receive the No-Ball Prize, and the Swedish Academy, which was to be made up entirely of hot broads, plus one spectacularly endowed young buck, would jump his bones from morning to night. The final scene would show him writing a novel while receiving a blow job from his chief rival, Joyce Carol Throats.

I arrived on the set the first day pumped with drugs.

"Action!" shouted Craig.

There was a knock at my hotel room door.

"Are you Ernest Hemingcock?" asked the gorgeous room-service girl, "the American writer who is here to receive the No-Ball Prize?"

"Why yes," I said.

"Are you also doing an article for a major American magazine on the pornography industry?"

"Yes," I said. "Yes I am."

"Well, then," she said, "let me help you with your research."

As her clothes melted away, I began to experience a certain satisfaction that can only be felt when one has achieved professional excellence. Moralists like to think that pornography is for the hoi polloi, but I see it differently now. Porn is fucking hot, and I love it. I will consume it, and star in it, any chance I get. It sure as hell beats watching the WB, or reading books. In that way, I thought, as three Swedish porn stars rammed dildos up my ass, I was totally, quintessentially, American.

(From *The Prisoner of Orgasm,* 1995)

THE SUBCOMANDANTE
RIDES AT DAWN

EPISODE ONE:
IN WHICH OUR HERO ARRIVES IN MEXICO, AND WITNESSES
AN APPALLING ACT OF CANNIBALISM

There is a wind blowing across Mexico, and like many Mexican winds, it has started a fire. This tempest was nurtured in the dignified breasts of the people, and has been around for a while. The blaze, on the other hand, sparked a little bit later, but still it burns, ripe and hot, with the promise of freedom. The wind is called revolution. The fire is called Esteban, for reasons I do not understand.

How will this noble wind make itself heard in these lands and across the country? How will this hidden fire burn, this Steve-flame that now crackles only in the mountains and canyons without yet descending to the valleys where money rules and lies govern?

There is no simple answer, and that's why I am here.

RECENTLY, I FOUND myself longing for Mexico City. My desire was poignant, yet somehow also abstract, since I had never actually been there. I tried to concoct excuses to travel to the city of my dreams, but could think of no possible junket, no flimsy pre-

THE NEAL POLLACK ANTHOLOGY OF AMERICAN LITERATURE

text other than my own wanderlust. Editors, regrettably, never go for that angle.

But a few days later, I was reading the *New York Times,* which I often find myself doing in the dawn's waning minutes. There was a small story on page 17 about an obscure group of indigenous rebels from the southern state of Chiapas who oppose the expropriation of their lands by oil and coffee conglomerates. They have named themselves Zapatistas, after Emiliano Zapatis, a legendary revolutionary figure from Mexican history. The article said that the Zapatistas were planning to visit Mexico City for some kind of protest and then they were going to return home in time for another protest. Immediately, my feature-writing antennae began to twitch. I called my editor, and then my pilot. I told him to gas up the plane; we were headed south.

Despite what I'd heard about Mexico City, my hotel room was not at all noisy, crowded, and chaotic. The private limousine ride from the airport was also comfortable, and relatively cheap. As soon as I arrived, I ate a delicious venison burger and read the only magazine article I'd been able to find about the Zapatistas, from *Die Humberschlingel,* an obscure German newsweekly.

It seemed the Zapatista leader was Subcomandante Marcos, an academic who had traveled to Chiapas and had been moved to revolution by the conditions of its poorest inhabitants. He wore a ski mask, smoked a pipe, and spoke in revolutionary language not heard in the United States since the early days of Woodrow Wilson's presidency. From his photos, he certainly seemed handsome, but I wondered why he hadn't sought more publicity for his cause.

To find out, I headed to the offices of Mexico's leading banking and natural-gas corporation, BanMexGasCo, for an interview with Emilio Cordoba Ruiz, executive vice president in charge of public relations. I found him in his office having an off-the-rack Zegna suit pressed while he was wearing it. He was also undergoing a pedicure, which he said was his third that day.

"Who is this Subcomandante Marcos?" I asked him.

He took a sip of his Pernod and water. His eyes narrowed.

"The subcomandante," he said, "is a vile, sister-fucking ver-min. He is a crusted piece of dung on the ass of the most wretched worm that crawls beneath the earth."

My notes read: "sister-fucking, dung, worm."

"According to a prominent German newsweekly," I said, "he is a popular hero."

"Let me ask you a question," he said. "What do you know about Mexico?"

I paused thoughtfully.

"Well," I said, "I saw *Treasure of the Sierra Madre.*"

He snickered.

"Then you know nothing."

He reached into a crystal candy bowl on his desk, pulled out a stubby, fleshy-looking morsel, and popped it in his mouth.

I stared at the bowl, and then at him.

"Are those human fingers?" I asked.

"That depends," he said, "on whether or not you consider Indians to be human."

It was then I realized that things in Mexico were not as they seemed.

EPISODE TWO:
IN WHICH OUR HERO IS ABDUCTED
BY A MYSTERIOUS MASKED BRIGADE

I awoke at dawn feeling refreshed, as I had gone to bed at three the previous afternoon. It was already a sunny, sooty day in Mexico City, and I was fit to explore. I hung my money pouch over my neck, put on a wide-brimmed straw hat and a new pair of khaki shorts, and left the hotel.

A handsome young man was hanging out in front, smoking a cigarette. He appeared to be intelligent enough.

"Excuse me," I said. "I am a wealthy American visitor who hasn't been to Mexico before. Do you know where I can see paint-ings by Diego Rivera?"

The man nearly swallowed his cigarette, which I found odd, but he recovered to smile at me.

"Rivera?" he said. "Certainly. Please, allow my friends and I to take you to his paintings in our very large, comfortable town car."

Well, wasn't that nice! I felt really lucky to have met such a helpful Mexican.

Five minutes later, the car pulled up, and I was inside. The man's friends, all four of them, were wearing ski masks. Oh, man, I thought. Luckier still.

"Hey," I said. "Are you guys Zapatistas?"

They all laughed ecstatically, for what seemed like an hour. I looked at my watch when they were done. It had, in fact, been an hour.

"Of course we are," said one of them, with a showy bow. "And I am the leader of the Zapatistas. Subcomandante Marcos. Perhaps you've heard of me."

I scrutinized the man.

"I have," I said, "but I hadn't realized that you were a dwarf."

Another man, red-faced with laughter, introduced himself as Subcomandante Julio. He said, "In order for you to hang out with the Zapatistas, we must have the PIN number of your automatic-teller card. For security reasons."

I expressed doubt, but the Dwarf-Marcos gave me a calming glass of mescal. After three more shots, I was gladly sharing with my Zapatista friends all kinds of confidential financial information, including several Condé Nast FedEx account numbers. We laughed and laughed as we drove around Mexico City, withdrawing money from various ATMs. I remember thinking, before the darkness overcame me: These guys are great! Man! What a party!

I awoke on a dirty sidewalk in the middle of a sprawling public market. My head felt like it had been stepped on by a mule, which it had.

The owner of the mule apologized and gave me a few pesos as restitution. This was fortunate, since all my money and identification were gone.

I bought a sandwich of puerco frito, or fried pork, and sat down in the street. In front of me, a hideous clown was juggling three zucchini, which he had set on fire. Later, a blind beggar came, carrying a guitar. He produced a wretched, mottled badger from his coat, and sang tuneless corridas as the animal shuffled pathetically along.

At that moment, Mexico was dreary. At least, I thought, the bandits hadn't found my reserve funds, the two thousand dollars that I always keep duct-taped inside my left buttock when I travel. Nope. That money would be right there . . .

Oh, shit.

I'd better call my editor.

EPISODE THREE:
IN WHICH OUR HERO BREATHES SOME MOUNTAIN AIR AND PURCHASES A LIVING CREATURE

The world was somewhat silent. Quiet it was, and not much to do on Saturday night. But there was a lake, as clear as bottled water. People would go down to the lake, sit by its edge, and ask it questions.

Why are we so bored?—said the people.

Because it is your fate—said the little lake.

We don't want to be here—said the people.

Fine, the lake said. That is your choice under the Mexican constitution. But be warned. When you come back, Germans will own businesses and things will be a lot more expensive. Also, I will be full of soap.

The people did not believe that this could happen, and they went to work at automotive plants and as gardeners in Los Angeles. Meanwhile, motorboats appeared on the lake.

Does anyone know where I can find some authentic native handicrafts?

I ONCE WROTE, before I ever visited Mexico, that San Cristobal de las Casas is "a beautiful colonial town in a temperate, pine-clad mountain atmosphere." But as I arrived in Chiapas, I realized that description didn't do the place fair. You wouldn't believe how temperate the weather was! I mean, it was really temperate.

Also, San Cristobal is just so cute. I saw the slogan "¡Ya Basta!" spray-painted everywhere. This, I guessed, translated as "We Got the Beat!" Mexico is so many years behind in pop culture, but I was encouraged that San Cristobal appeared to have a thriving rock scene.

In my first two days in San Cristobal, I ate at the Bagel Barn, went to a Kate Winslet film festival, and danced all night at the Jolly Roger Mountain Discotecque. San Cristobal may have been the site of the first Zapatista rebellion in January 1994, but the only evidence of the event that I found was in the gift shops, which sold Zapatista dolls, T-shirts, and a Subcomandante Marcos jack-in-the-box that sprang up at the end of "The Internationale."

I was disappointed that I didn't run into any revolutionaries, but was thrilled to encounter three guys who had a huge stash of that magical Oaxacan weed, marijuana. One night we sat in my hotel room, smoked out, and traded travel stories. Mitch from San Francisco had lain in a hammock for seven consecutive days. Martin, a British computer programmer, had been on a bus in Guatemala that got a flat tire. Bernard, a French stilt-walker, had slept with a Honduran prostitute who kept pet chickens.

Latin America, we all agreed, was extraordinary.

We became hungry, so we ventured to find some ice cream. Several Mayans were in the *zocalo,* performing a traditional dance for an applauding group of American tourists. How fortunate, I thought, for us to encounter a spontaneous display of culture.

Then a young woman with dirty blond braids was in my face. Her nose was pierced in seven different places. She wore men's pants of a Guatemalan design. Hanging from her neck was an adorable little pookie bear of a baby.

"Oh, man," she said. "I am like so totally hungry."

"You speak English!" I said.

"Duh," she said. "I'm from Oregon. Listen. I'm totally broke. Do you wanna buy my baby?"

I thought she was kidding, and so did the guys I was with. We all began making baby noises.

"How much?" I asked.

"Twenty bucks."

Suddenly, her offer didn't seem so absurd. Twenty bucks for a baby was cheap! Why, in the States, he would have cost at least a thousand dollars.

I have always found it difficult to refuse a bargain.

"Aren't you a cutie?" I said, as she handed me the baby.

Quickly, she was gone, and so were my buddies. I realized the magnitude of what I had done. I had purchased a baby, albeit an American one, while I was stoned in Mexico. This was going to make investigative reporting very difficult for the rest of my stay.

We went back to my room, and I tried to fall asleep. The kid, who I'd placed in the soft part of my suitcase, began to cry, softly at first, then more plaintively.

"Mama!" he wailed. "MAAAAA! MAAAA!"

I guessed he was hungry, but I didn't have anything in the room but beer.

Outside, there was a sound, far, far off. Was that sound revolution?

It was hard to tell.

EPISODE FOUR:
IN WHICH OUR HERO ENCOUNTERS SCENES
OF APPALLING RURAL POVERTY

The sign at the military guard post read, "Welcome to the Lacandon Jungle: Population 0." That number seemed hard for me to trust.

I exited my Jeep, which I'd rented for the day for only $550. The federale on duty was a slovenly teen. He slouched in a metal chair, taking potshots at armadillos with his machine gun.

"Good morning!" I said. "Mind if I play through?"

"No visitors," he said, somewhat mechanically, as he extinguished a possum with a spray of bullets. "An exception can be made only if you are an instructor from the School of the Americas headed to the outskirts of Santa Pendejo to train the leaders of the counterinsurgency movement."

I sensed an opening, although I wished I were familiar with this School of the Americas.

"Why yes, I am," I said. "Can't wait for the counterinsurgency!"

He rose, with reluctance, and looked into my car. My newly purchased son was in the passenger seat, cooing and chewing on a banana peel.

"Why do you have a baby?" said the guard.

I thought quickly.

"His mom had to work," said I.

SANTA PENDEJO IS one of numerous "Autonomous Communities" that exist throughout Chiapas. Its five hundred or so inhabitants have established their own school, their own medical clinic, their own town hall, and a nifty little bistro with a decent selection of mid-priced Chilean wines.

Nevertheless, they are poor, and it shows. Their one-room houses are made of red clay and potato-chip bags. Some of them sleep in trees. One elderly man lives entirely in a wheelbarrow.

Fortunately, the town hall is equipped with cable television, so I had something to do. I spent an evening flipping through the stations with Felipe, who, as mayor, gets to sit in Santa Pendejo's only luxury recliner.

"What's on the Independent Film Channel?" I asked.

Felipe sighed.

"Señor," he said, "we do not receive the Independent Film Channel here."

Oh, God.

Someone has to help these people!

MY BEST FRIEND in Santa Pendejo is named Ramon. He is about my age, even though he has never attended Harvard. One night, we sat on a log in the jungle, listening to the screams of a thousand monkeys, watching the moonlight reflect on the lush foliage, and drinking a mammoth bottle of mescal.

"It is so hard for us here," he said. "We work always, but receive nothing in return."

"I know what you mean," I said. "One time, I stayed up all night producing a segment of *60 Minutes,* and then they forgot to mention my name in the credits."

Later, we lay on the ground, in a state of what they called, at Exeter, extreme inebriation. I took a swig of booze and put the bottle to my baby's lips, since he had developed a taste for the hard stuff.

"You know what I wish?" Ramon said.

"What?"

"That I was making it with a really hot chick right now, one with blond hair and incredibly large breasts."

"My girlfriend, back in the States, is like that," I said. "Only she has no hair."

We heard a rustling in the distance that slowly grew to a thunder. The jungle appeared to be cleaving itself in twain before our eyes. The noise grew clearer: a clomping of hooves, a whooshing of machetes.

A fiery stallion burst through the bush. Upon him sat a ski-masked man, smoking a pipe.

He shouted: "Neoliberalism, the doctrine that makes it possible for stupidity and cynicism to govern in diverse parts of the earth, does not allow for inclusion other than that of subjection to genocide!"

I turned to Ramon.

"Who's this joker?" I said.

EPISODE FIVE:
IN WHICH OUR HERO LEARNS
THE MEANING OF REVOLUTION

The cold is harsh in these mountains. Fortunately, I am wearing Polarfleece, and Subcomandante Marcos, my interview subject, is wearing his masks. My baby is wrapped in husks of corn.

"You will join the guerrillas," says the subcomandante. "We have no use for interviews."

"But the world must know about you and your cause!" I exclaim.

"They can read our Web page," he says.

Oh, no.

"You have a Web page?"

"Yes," he says. "We are international heroes and have been written about thousands of times. What of you? Do you think we're bandits?"

I blink my flashlight on and off, out of nervousness and disgust. We are in the subcomandante's private headquarters, and I am blindfolded. It is difficult to take notes. But I suppose it no longer matters, since I no longer carry the illusion that I have a scoop.

"I . . . I don't know," I say. "Why are you not talking?"

"Because," he says, "I am eating a grapefruit."

He tells me about the times of Zapata and Villa and the revolution and the land and the injustice and hunger and ignorance and sickness and repression and everything.

"Wow," I say. "Only I don't know who this Pancho Villa character is."

He sighs, and my lesson truly begins.

SUBCOMANDANTE MARCOS IS there, inside my mind. He is so charismatic and powerful. I can feel the tug of revolution in my breast. But I must remain objective. I must.

Our interviews continue.

"Do you know," he says, "that for every dollar we earn in Chiapas, the oil industry makes one billion dollars in profit?"

"No!"

"Do you know that half our young people don't know how to drive?"

"That's terrible!"

"Do you know that soldiers cut off our fingers because

midlevel bureaucrats in Mexico City consider them a delicacy?"

Of everything I have seen and heard in my five days in Mexico, this hits me hardest of all, right where I live, and in my gut, too.

"I have seen this happen," I say, "and it makes me angry."

"Then join us!" he says. "Join the National Zapatista Liberation Army!"

"I want to, but I can't. See, I've got this opportunity to get a piece in 'Talk of the Town,' and . . ."

The subcomandante puts his finger to my lips, and gently strokes my hair. I feel warm and confused. He removes my blindfold, and walks over to the far wall, where he pushes a button. The wall slides away to reveal an elaborate pipe organ, in the Baroque style. I feel myself in a swoon. The subcomandante sits down at the organ, and, without removing his mask, begins to sing.

Night-time sharpens, heightens each sensation . . .
Darkness stirs and wakes imagination . . .
Silently the senses abandon their defenses . . .

His magnificent tenor voice haunts me, as though I had been hearing it my entire life. The subcomandante is penetrating the sweet, thorny labyrinth of my heart, and I cannot resist.

Softly, deftly, music shall caress you . . .
Hear it, feel it, secretly possess you.
Open up your mind, let your fantasies unwind,
in this darkness, which you know, you cannot fight—
the darkness of the music of the night . . .
You alone can make my song take flight—
help me make the music of the night . . .

"Oh Subcomandante!" I shout. "I have waited for you all my years!"

He rises, sweeps over to me, and takes me in his arms.

"Then you are prepared to ride with me at dawn?"

"Yes! Yes! I will do anything for you!" I say. "I love you more than anything that ever was."

The tree of life knows that, whatever happens, the warm music surrounding it will never stop. Whoever dies, whoever suffers from infernal wounds, music will create love as long as men and women plow the earth and breathe the air. And as the subcomandante takes me, kisses me, makes me his as I make him mine, I know that I have left behind my worldly concerns and joined the magic of eternity. I belong to the subcomandante. Forever.

"But what about my baby?" I ask, later. After. "Can we take my baby?"

"He is our baby now, little judio," says my subcomandante. "He belongs to the revolution. He will grow strong and fierce, not to mention intelligent and sexy. And we shall name him Che!"

Yes. Che it will be, a hero's name.

Che Pollack.

(From *The Last Days of Capitalism,* 1994)

ONE WRITER'S ROUTINE

In March 1999, my Swiss girlfriend reluctantly persuaded me to contribute to the New York Times's *"Writers on Writing" column. My contribution follows.*

It is evening here, and with the waning wispy light come sounds. The forest brims with the hoots and rustles of creatures beyond imagining, invisible mammals of the night and their avian sidekicks, unwitting beneficiaries of my successful anti-highway-development campaigns in this secluded county. Across the bay, where the fish leap and trickle in the lushness of my forced overstock, a final purply blaze sparkles atop Mount Winchester, whose peak is still covered by the spring's last desperate snow.

I admire the remnants of my goat-cheese-and-porcini ravioli, and feel both serene with knowledge and anxious in anticipation of Roger's magnificent braised rabbit loin, which he always serves with a huckleberry coulis and herbed balsamic polenta cake. As always, between courses, I begin to write. For write I must, as dictated by a cruel god, a crueler agent, and my public, cruelest, and yet kindest, of all.

It was not always so. In those spry days before I became this prizewinning rustic, this dotard, this paragon of arcadian selfhood, my life was unencumbered by schedule. I could write a chapter in an hour and still have time for Coltrane over dinner, the actual, physical Coltrane, who wrote "Giant Steps" for me, his favorite thing. Then came the years with drugs, and Vietnam, and my bitter public divorce, followed by a close bid for the Maryland governor's mansion. But now I find myself here, by the mountains, and the water, and the ancient woods. I have settled, at last, into routine.

These preceding five-odd years were productive ones. I wrote three novels, a history of the Middle East, and a volume of jokes about professional baseball. I had experienced periods of equal fecundity in the past, but never with such focus, or with such a gifted cook at my behest. I owe all to my special regimen, which I will now share with you in the spirit of writing well. The days do vary slightly; at times I dine with luminaries brighter than the sexual potentates listed here. Nonetheless, as my dear friend Burroughs once said: Never quit. Never stop writing. And never lend money to a federal agent—but that is advice for another day.

4 A.M.: Snap awake with first hint of dawn. Remember mother.

4:30 A.M.: Coffee. Rouse Roger for massage.

5 A.M.: Swim bay with improbable speed. Two hundred sit-ups. Oatmeal-cranberry scone.

6 A.M.: Write as though possessed by all three Furies. Shove towel in door crack. Scream, "Why is there so much noise in the world?" Write more.

9 A.M.: Engage in spirited E-mail exchange with assistant books editor of *Slate.*

9:45 A.M.: Wield pen as Jove would wield thunderbolt, only with more wit and finesse.

11:45 A.M.: Crumble onto couch. Descend into pit of mental blackness and despair as wicked storm cloud of grief and doubt envelops soul. Ponder suicide and eternal sojourn in hell.

12:30 P.M.:   Lunch.

1:45 P.M.:   Take perfectly ripe dessert peach into maple grove. Enjoy tender juice as it runs down cheek. Play guitar. Sleep.

2:30 P.M.:   Exchange bitter recriminatory E-mail with Christopher Hitchens.

3 P.M.:   Write as though cannibal Huns were beating down door with hatchet. Write more. *More, dammit!*

6 P.M.:   Curse self briefly. Pour Glenlivet for cursed self.

6:30 P.M.:   Phone conversation with former drug czar Barry McCaffrey. Assure him that all is proceeding according to design.

7:15 P.M.:   Guests arrive for dinner. Tell anecdotes about Anaïs Nin to put them in proper mood. Yell, "Roger, you half-wit! Where are my venison chops?"

9 P.M.:   Produce hookah. Talk of stolen days in Turkey.

10 P.M.:   Make love to woman from Brazil, Montreal, Villareal, or Israel. It matters not where, as long as place ends in "l."

11 P.M.:   Offer woman crackers. Kick her out of bed for eating them. Write for solid half hour, without feminine interruption.

11:45 P.M.:   Conduct pithy Instant-Message exchange with Garrison Keillor.

12:15 A.M.:   See shadowy visage of Wally Trumbull, former roommate at Exeter, over bed. Tell Wally that soon you will be joining him in sylvan eternal pastures of heaven.

12:30 A.M.: Brain ends daily roil. At last, chaste, perfect, unstained sleep. Good night, my darling genius. Good night.

2:30 A.M.: Roger shoots himself in head, but, as usual, doesn't die. Mop up blood and put him back to bed with aspirin. Resolve to write piece about strange domestic situation for *Times* Weekend section.

4 A.M.: Wake self up. Brush self off. Start all over again.

WHY AM I SO HANDSOME?

PART ONE: FROM OHIO TO ENGLAND

People who know me, and many who do not, are familiar with my talents. They have read of my calculating intelligence, my vast web of connections, my deserved reputation as a white-hot dance-floor dynamo. They never question my immense journalistic output, and never want to, because my stuff is so astoundingly good.

Like Don Quixote, I am symbolic of many essential human dilemmas. But no matter how much people ponder me—no matter how much I ponder myself—one question remains vexingly unanswered.

Why am I so handsome?

IT ALL STARTED when I was twelve years old, and prematurely muscular. My brother Elvin took me to a local club known for its impossibly strong drinks and "Special Couch Room," which held mysterious secrets.

"You're too young to go in there," Elvin said. "Besides, you have to be invited."

Fifteen minutes into the show, a bald mocha-colored behemoth approached. He was wearing golden hoops in either ear, and electric-green stretch pants, which didn't look as bad as they sound. He handed me a note.

"The owner of this establishment invites you to join her on the Secret Couch," it read. "There you will learn the lovemaking skills necessary for you to become a successful magazine writer."

"I think this is for you," I said to Elvin.

"No!" the behemoth bellowed. "Send the little one. The owner wants the little one."

That night as she splayed me on chenille, I may have lost my virginity, but she nearly lost her mind. Her orgasms, of a type with which I would soon become familiar, deafened, thundered, established an epoch. Mercy, I thought. I had better harness this power, and quickly, or else someone might die.

"Oh," she moaned. "You are so handsome!"

Yes, yes, I thought. But why?

MY FRIEND CARRIE, who is a professional comedian, knows the lead tenor for the Lyric Opera of Chicago, who, curiously, was my roommate at Exeter. He, in turn, is friendly with Jacques Pepin, who once shared a taxi with my father's butler on the way to a party thrown for the Brazilian novelist Jorge Amado, where he met Nate Dogg, who in turn introduced him to Conan O'Brien, who got Carrie on his show, where she met Tom Selleck, who later took her out for drinks with several other famous people and was a perfect gentleman when, bombed off her noodle, she attempted to chew on his mustache.

Isn't that interesting? Someday, I will write a whole article about the incident, involving science. I will probably win an award.

At the moment, however, I am on a per diem in Cambridge, England, where I have previously been both a student and a guest lecturer in the political-science department. In particular, I am visiting Monica Carruthers, head of the Cambridge Institute of Physical Appearance Studies and the world's leading researcher on the topic at hand.

Like most female scientists, Monica wears thin-framed, demure glasses and keeps her hair in an austere but not inappropriate bun that she once spray-painted mustard yellow, entirely by accident. She is twenty-nine, but looks twenty-seven. She is such a thorough scientist that from time to time she speaks only in numbers, and everyone around her falls asleep.

When I enter Monica's lab, she is carefully examining two hedgehogs. One is certainly more handsome than the other, as I point out.

"Well, yes," she says. "In certain animal species, handsome individuals begin to distinguish themselves at birth, and . . ."

I'm getting closer to the answer. But then, almost unconsciously, Monica undoes her hair and removes her glasses.

"And why?" I say.

"I'm sorry," she says. "Did you say something?"

"No."

She slinks toward me, drapes onto my stern, muscular neck.

"You must forgive me," she says. "But you are just so fucking handsome."

I used to think that if I talked to enough researchers, I would discover the truth about my good looks. I would be not merely handsome, but an encyclopedia of handsomeness. Instead, Monica is the fourth scientist this week with whom I've had sex, yet I've learned absolutely nothing. It looks like I will have to do what journalists have done since the dawn of journalism, dozens of years ago.

I will have to go to Africa.

PART TWO: CAMEROON

The moment I get off the airplane, I am bathed in a warm glaze of equatorial sweat. No, wait. Some damn punk-ass kid has just dumped a bucket of water on my head.

After enduring the mockery of several unkind security guards, I acquire a guide at the baggage claim. His name, he tells me, is Louis Rukeyser.

THE NEAL POLLACK ANTHOLOGY OF AMERICAN LITERATURE

"That's odd," I say, "for an African."

"Yes," he says. "My mother was a great fan of *Wall $treet Week.*"

Oh, Lord, I am tired. I have come to Africa in search of iboga, a mythical, but very real, hallucinogen that is distilled from the bark of a tree which has an orange fruit and a yellow flower and is believed by many sacred tribal priests to be a direct pipeline to the spirit world and which can heal the sick. Also, some people in the States believe it is a certain cure for heroin addiction.

Like I care. I just want to get stoned and learn why I am so handsome.

I ask Louis if he can score me some. He tells me that his cousin Kondracke happens to be a chieftain who conducts iboga-eating ceremonies for curious Westerners with five hundred dollars to burn.

"But for you," he says, "the drug is free."

I think, "Bitchin'!" But I ask, "Why?"

"The iboga ceremony is like love," Louis says. "Iboga eaters are one with the earth, and the sky, and the moon fills our hearts with joy when we eat it. Also, you are a very good-looking man."

I can't remember the last time I paid for drugs.

I HAD REACHED a point in my New York life where I felt spiritually detached, morally stunted, psychically neutered. For the last six years, I had done nothing but write about myself, and the well was running dry.

After seven days of pondering where all the flowers have gone, I leave my hotel room. Louis is waiting exactly where I'd left him, in the lobby. Man, is this guy loyal.

"Cousin Kondracke has been waiting," he says.

I expect a voyage of at least several hours through dense jungle, since there is no other kind. I intend to see jaguars and snakes and the conducting of paramilitary drills. In my mind, Kondracke sits on a throne of bamboo, fanned by eight or ten of his three hundred wives, chewing on the shank of a mythical beast. I have a backpack full of beads and wine and blue jeans and bootleg music videos to give in offering. I am prepared to bow before him, and, if not kiss, at least touch his feet.

Louis takes me to a conference room decorated with photographs of the president of Cameroon and Kevin Costner, who are friends. At the end of the table sits a modest bureaucrat in a gray suit, playing Minesweeper on his laptop computer. This, Louis says, is Kondracke.

"YOU WISH TO PARTAKE OF THE SACRED IBOGA?" Kondracke asks.

"Yes," I say.

The chief scrutinizes my expensive safari clothes and tells me to remove my pith helmet.

"Last night," he says, "I dreamt that an astoundingly handsome American journalist would visit my conference room and defeat me at Tetris. Now it appears that the prophecy will be fulfilled."

Kondracke produces a coconut half from his briefcase and fills it with a white powder, which he then tops off with a shot of tequila and about half a can of Sprite. I know I am about to eat my first iboga. Whenever I think about the taste afterward, I am reminded that Sprite and Tequila don't really mix.

"ARE YOU ENJOYING THE IBOGA?" Kondracke says. "IT IS REALLY VERY SACRED."

"Quit it," says Louis.

For the first few seconds, I feel nothing.

Then I vomit into Louis's lap, and he slaps me hard across the mouth. Kondracke holds a mirror before me. I can see my Brooklyn apartment, clearly, and all the women with whom I've had sex. The phone is ringing with another magazine assignment. God. I cannot endure the pressure any longer.

Six minutes later, it seems that the drug's effects have ceased, except that I feel a little tingly and Kondracke is dancing on the table with a stuffed gorilla, both of them wearing bowler hats. Louis sleeps peacefully in the corner, thumb in mouth, dreaming of a better life.

Whoa. Hang on. My face appears in the mirror. It shifts, molds, stretches. It bounces up and down. It changes every few seconds, in claymation. The whirl of images will at last release the answer to my question from the depths of my soul or from the very heights of heaven!

Then the trip ends.

And still I am handsome.

PART THREE: NEW YORK

I walk the streets of a New York that is not the New York I know, yet is still definitely New York, or at least I think so. For instance, I don't recall Greenwich Village having cobblestone streets or an Earl Scruggs Taco House with a winking neon pig in front, and while I am used to the male prostitutes on Bleecker Street saying "hiya, foxy" as I pass, they generally don't have polar-bear heads. Also, why is a twenty-foot-wide balloon of Mayor Giuliani floating above me, without, seemingly, the aid of strings?

"New York," I sigh. "You never know what to expect."

It is night, or noon, or some other time during the day. I see that my old college roommate, Hendrik Tolliver, is playing the autoharp at the Zazu Pitts Cabaret and Cafeteria. Strange, I think, since Hendrik has been in a Peruvian prison since 1976 on a trumped-up asthma-medicine-smuggling charge.

I duck into the club, which, naturally, is below ground, and order a Scotch, neat. The bartender asks for five dollars.

"Oh my God!" I cry. "I left my wallet in my gym locker, and I'm going to fail all my finals!"

"That's okay," says the bartender. "Your credit's good here."

"But I've never been here before—"

Before I can finish, he disappears through a hole in the floor. I turn toward the stage. Yep. There's Hendrik, playing "Lady Sings the Blues" for a group of Japanese businessmen, my grandmother, and the cast of *Knots Landing.* I gulp the Scotch in one swallow and wait for him to come over, which he does immediately.

"I'm playing for a party later," he says, "and it's going to be a hot one."

Good old Hendrik! He always had the hookup. He hands me the address, which is printed on a poppy-seed bagel.

"How the hell am I going to get to White Plains without a car?" I ask.

"You can fly," he says, "with me."

"Don't be ridiculous," I say. "There's no way—"

We are already in the air, soaring over the Chrysler Building.

"Hendrik," I ask, "why am I so handsome?"

But he cannot answer me, for he has become a bird.

WE LAND AT a mansion, which is just like the one in *Citizen Kane,* only this one is made of cheese and staffed by men in togas and Walter Winchell masks. At the door, one of them takes my coat and stuffs it into a trash compactor.

I am suddenly aware of music. Actually, I'm aware of a single annoying piano note, being played continuously. It simply has to cease.

"DONG! DONG! DONG! DONG!"

I enter a circular room, tastefully done in blond wood, green linoleum, and rugs bearing my likeness. The room is dimly lit, almost not lit at all, and that piano note just keeps clinking away. In the center of the room stands a man in a long black robe and a Grover mask. Around him are thirteen other men, each in a robe, masked as different characters from *Sesame Street.* In a larger circle around them are twenty-eight women, all spectacularly beautiful, each one a different color.

The men begin to chant, sonorously.

"Rub a dub dub! Thanks for the grub! Yay, God!"

The women chant back:

"Amen, brother! Get on board that soul train!"

Suddenly, Sydney Pollack approaches me from behind. "You must leave at once," he hisses. "You are too handsome to be here. The other men will get jealous!" Then a butler hits him over the head with a Genoa salami, and he dies.

By now, the ceremony has moved into an antechamber. The women splay on tables and couches of various shapes. The piano continues to clang.

"DONG! DONG! DONG!"

The men hover over the women, doing hideous things to them. I cannot tell what exactly, because digitally enhanced shadow figures are blocking my view. From the sounds I hear, the women are not enjoying themselves, but the men are.

"DONG!"

My tolerance has ended.

I shout: "This is the most boring orgy ever! And will somebody smash that goddamn piano?"

The men whip around. The high priest rips off his Grover mask to reveal a completely average-looking face. The other men do the same, and believe me, they're nothing special either.

"Kill him!" they shout. "Kill the handsome man!"

They advance on me bearing pitchforks and burning torches. The screams of the beautiful women can't save me. In fact, they only make the men more jealous, and as I dash across the muddy grounds, pursued by a homely mob, I realize that I am about to die. I am falling, falling, falling, into the end.

THE LIMOUSINE DROPS me off at my apartment building, which is made entirely of marble, at dawn. It was such a long night, and I am so tired, and I wish I knew what happened to my shoes.

My mail is waiting for me in the foyer. Oh, yuck: *The Nation*'s Spring Books issue and a postcard from Aunt Ruth. Not much of a mail day, I fear.

In the kitchen, Nicole Kidman is cooking me breakfast. I pinch myself to see if I am dreaming, but then I remember that I'm married to her, at least for the time being.

"We have to tell each other everything," she says as she passes me a joint, later, in bed.

"Yes," I say, "everything."

She begins to weep.

"What is it, my little koala bear?" I ask.

"Nothing," she says. "I was just thinking how lucky I am to have such a handsome husband."

The next day, as we embrace in a toy store, sobbing passionately, she says, "There is something we have to do."

"What is it, kangaroo face?" I ask.

She says, "We have to clean out the refrigerator."

A single piano note plays again. Enormous stuffed hippopotamuses surround me. But the reality of marriage subverts all fantasies. Of course, this is the end.

(From *Listening to Silence*, 1991)

THE FIRST ANNUAL
NEW YORK UNIVERSITY
NEAL POLLACK CHAIR IN
AMERICAN LITERATURE
LECTURE

Good evening, friends, acolytes, students, and citizens of New York. My name is Neal Pollack. I am the Greatest Living American Writer. Tonight, I begin my nationwide speaking tour to tell the young people of America how I claimed that title, held on to it, and gradually codified it through a savvy mixture of corporate synergy and brutal, bone-crushing all-star wrestling action. You are fortunate to be present at the fragrant dawn of a great literary lecture series.

Naturally, because of my exalted status and because of the extra-high level of pheromones I exude, women and men of various levels of attractiveness often ask me questions, both when I am on airplanes and on the street. The questions can be lumped into two general categories. One, Will you please make love to me, preferably in the next fifteen minutes? Two, How did you arrive at your current position atop the Mount McKinley of American letters?

To the first question, my answer is Yes, of course I will have sex with you, but let me check my voice mail first. The second answer is more complicated, though I generally tell people that it is easy to become successful if you put naked pictures of yourself on the Internet, read your E-mail every five minutes, and have wealthy, prominent friends who find you amusing.

The unsatisfied and the wicked then ask why I pursue the literary life; perhaps also how, but why most of all, and they ask correctly. As you know, I have lost many friends and contracted several venereal diseases during my current ascent to the top of this ladder of words, but the hidden costs of fame are more than outweighed by its outrageous benefits. Whereas two years ago I was an ordinary journalist, a mere gutter striver in a provincial Grub Street of the soul, I am now Dolly Parton's best friend. People from the Netherlands want to interview me. I have become a homeowner, a boat owner, and part owner of the United States Basketball League. But none of these, while certainly juicy perks, are reasons in themselves.

No, I became a writer for one simple reason: I am in love with literature.

I love the way it feels against my skin and the way it smells in the morning before it showers, the way the sunlight makes its hair gleam in the crisp, clean Colorado sunshine, its little literary laugh, and the way it also knows when I'm sad and when I need a neck rub. Any sacrifice in the world is not enough to sustain a love like the one I have for literature, a love that has been hard fought, hard won, and hard to hold.

Literature and I met at a pool hall on the Lower East Side, a place named for a famous painter who is now dead. It was hanging out with its friends art and music, and I was hanging out with Benicio del Toro and Derek Jeter. Our eyes locked immediately.

"So," said literature, "what have you been reading?"

"I've been reading you all my life," I said.

From there, our friends faded into a fuzzy background montage. I complained to literature about the difficulty of being a freelance magazine writer in New York, about its uncaring world of deadlines and insipid service journalism, and literature understood. Literature told me about an installation it was doing at a performance space in Williamsburg, and invited me to come along to a party, which would have a Brazilian DJ, go-go dancers, and a good number of VH-1 employees dressed, somewhat ironically, as genetically modified sheep.

From there, we whirled in the winds of romance. I took literature to Prospect Park to watch authentic Caribbean-Americans participate in their lunch-eating rituals. Literature took me to a poetry slam in the Bronx, where the sidewalks are alive with the words of the people. We ate cilantro-flavored cellophane noodles for days on end. When we kissed, it was usually against the iron fence of an East Village church, and our bodies tingled with significance.

One morning, literature and I lay in bed, smoking. We had been up shooting heroin much of the night, and we were spent.

"I need some money," literature said.

"Baby, we don't need money," I said. "We got each other."

"Fuck you," said my love, "I need some fucking money NOW!"

Literature had revealed its dark side. I spent days walking from Fifty-third Street to Fifty-seventh Street and back again, trying to sell my paperback rights. Sometimes, I even ventured down to Chelsea, for coffee. And each day, I would come home with nothing more than a residual check in hand.

Literature was usually lying on the floor wrapped in a filthy-smelling blanket. My apartment was strewn with garbage and bits of sculpture, long abandoned. No one had done dishes in weeks. The cats howled with hunger. Obviously, something had to give.

"Listen, babe," I said, "why don't we get away for a few days."

Toby Wolff had rented a house on Cape Cod with the editors of the *New York Times Book Review* and had invited us to come along. I told literature that the air would be good for both of us, and also Rick Bass would be there for a few days.

"I don't need any fucking air," said literature. "I need money, and I need drugs."

That night, while literature slept off a pint of Mad Dog, I stuffed all its belongings into a bag that I'd received for judging the documentary competition at Sundance. I lifted literature off my bed. I could not believe how much weight it had lost since those heady, early days, when the world was young and we met Lou Reed for lunch once a week. Gently, I placed literature and its possessions in the hall, and called to have my locks changed. In the morning, I could hear the pounding and the screams, followed by the rapping and the whispers, and then nothing.

You may say my behavior was cruel, and it certainly was that and more. But there was no way I was going to let my love for literature ruin my literary career. I had too much pride, and too much ambition, for that.

I still keep my love right here, in my breast pocket, next to my National Book Critics Circle Award. It is always with me, and always an inspiration. Still, the day I let literature go was the day I became a writer for real. And if you really love literature, you will do the same, because from the burning fire of our literary passions, the world will be created anew, perceptions of time and space will be forever altered, or at least we will get invited to Bread Loaf and Yaddo and make a few thousand bucks as visiting professors at Carleton College.

This, then, is my message to you.

(From *Notes and Noodlings,* 1963)

WITNESS FOR THE
REVOLUTION

In the warm months, I would leave my office for a half hour or so and take a hired car to Washington Square Park. There I removed my shoes, breathed peaceably, and sipped on raspberry-flavored mineral water until I burped. Soon it became my habit to rat out Rastafarian drug dealers to the bike cops, and I became a known and feared presence. The freaks would scatter to the wind when I appeared.

I was unimaginably successful and wealthy, and my feet inexorably pumped the pedals of progress. Occasionally, in the few free seconds available to me, I would think, for some reason, about a line from a book I hadn't read in college, about the masses of men and their lives of quiet desperation, but I could never understand how that applied to me. I was, temporarily, the editor in chief of an E-commerce magazine with several hundred thousand readers. My life was neither quiet nor desperate.

One afternoon, as I sunned myself, a young woman approached my bench. She had blond dreadlocks that came down past her shoulders and confident blue eyes that seemed to sing a deep, rousing, significant chorus. She wore black jeans and a T-shirt bearing a cartoon of Leon Trotsky preparing to sodomize Mickey Mouse on a Cuban beach.

"Have you heard of the Revolutionary Communist Party?" she asked.

She handed me a copy of a newspaper that literally was black and white and red all over. Its front page bore an angry headline, thirty-six-point Palatino, and a photograph of law-enforcement officials, heavily armed, beating several young Asian types bloody. At first the prose seemed didactic and confusing, but after several articles, it began to make rhythmic sense, and I was increasingly entranced. I talked to the woman for several minutes, and then for several hours. For the first time in nearly three years, I missed the market's closing bell. But by then, I had already become convinced that profit, and all it represented, was evil, and it was wrong.

Her name was Kim.

When she left me in the park that evening after rejecting my attempt to fondle her breasts, I returned to my East Village duplex and began cleaning my soul. I gave three of my four suits and a rotating Shower Massage nozzle to the guy in the bodega on Avenue C, and donated my Palm Pilot to a homeless shelter in Yonkers. Soon, all I had left was a backpack of casual clothes and a copy of *Rules for Radicals* by Saul Alinsky, which I had stolen from Barnes & Noble.

I rose one morning at 9 A.M., and kissed my wife on the forehead.

"Where the hell are you going?" she asked.

"I must organize the people," I said.

As I thumbed a ride on the Brooklyn Bridge, I wiped away the fog of materialism and doubt that had plagued me since I first cleared a million, back in January, or maybe March. Kim was perfectly correct, and some day I would possess her. Oh, yes.

The only solution *was* Communist Revolution.

IN A BROWNING, expansive field, behind a salmon-processing plant and a shoe factory, cosseted between two sewage canals located on the steaming edge of the San Fernando Valley, I came upon a tin-and-sandpaper hut. Seventeen men were living there, sleeping three to a single bed, gathered around a grass-burning stove and a thirty-five-inch television set. All of them were Mexican, all illegal, all employed in seasonal agriculture. Here, I determined, the struggle would commence.

Because of my counterinsurgency work in Nicaragua in the 1980s, my Spanish was excellent. I spoke to these fellows of the imminent overthrow of capitalism.

"Your labor is exploited to ensure a profit from the exchange of goods for the investor of money," I said.

They ignored me. Soccer was on television. Several of them were drinking beer and listening to Santana on a small but effective stereo system. Others amused themselves by playing the Spanish-language version of Scattergories.

I said: "Don't you want to control the means of your own production? Envision with me a classless, collectivist order without money or hierarchical work structures! Embrace a new world!"

There was silence, so I began clapping rhythmically.

"Motivate, people! Motivate! Get psyched for the revolution!"

"Please be quiet," said one of the men near the TV. "This is a playoff game. Also, we are already members of the United Farm Workers and are paid adequately. We live here to save money for our children in Mexico. We don't require your help."

These naive trabajadores had no idea what they were doing. They couldn't understand that unions are but a mild evolutionary step toward the final workers' paradise.

I slumped toward the door. From a dark corner of the shack stepped a small, determined-looking man. He had a mustache and a kind, modestly round face.

"For you, I will travel to the ends of the earth, and Delaware, too," he said. "Also, I will carry your bags."

"Sir," I gasped, "pray tell, what is your name?"

"They call me Pancho Sanza."

A humble manservant had been delivered unto me.

PANCHO AND I arrived in Las Vegas on an optimistic morning in mid-October. Walking from L.A. had taken time, sure, but since

Pancho was now lifting my pack, it was possible for me to think importantly. The revolution, I decided, would begin in Nevada, where America reinvented itself on a weekly, daily, hourly basis. Once a sleepy desert hamlet, then a mob and swingers' hideaway, now a corporate entertainment state, Vegas was ready for the next stage of its evolution. I was determined to make it a haven for Communists everywhere.

We got a room at the Westward Ho, one of the old-school hotels, a place for the people that also served ninety-nine-cent margaritas, which served as a necessary salve to the omnipresence of the desert sun. By noon we were drunk like everyone else, and we took to the Strip.

At the entrance to Caesar's Palace's Forum Shops, we encountered a group of six Delta Chis from Iowa State University.

"Hello," I said. "Would you like to help us establish communal banks through which people can exchange products and labor, thereby eliminating all state and capitalist institutions?"

"No," they said.

It was on to the dancing waters of the Bellagio, which took us six hours to reach on foot as the hordes gathered to engage in their useless hedonistic enterprise. We met sisters from Cleveland, aged eighteen, twenty-three, and thirty-five, all named Sue, who were on a girls' weekend. They had thus far each lost about twenty dollars at the tables.

"We don't really gamble," said a Sue.

"Pancho and I would like to abolish private property altogether," I said.

"God," said another. "Why?"

They disgusted me with their pointless world of flappy oversized tennis shorts and bright-pink tank tops, of middle-level managers dropping their pathetic stashes of quarters into jungle-themed digital slot machines. America's citizens were soft and weak. A good work camp would fix them all.

"You will die in the unholy inferno of collective catharsis!" I shouted. "Fuck you all!"

Someone spun me around, and Pancho spun beside me. I found myself facing a middle-aged African-American in madras shorts and a Colorado Rockies T-shirt.

"Don't talk like that," he said. "I've got kids here."

"Come on, brother," I said. "Your people need to join the revolution!"

"No way," he said. "I've got a good job in Vegas, and so does my wife, and we send our kids to a well-funded, integrated suburban school."

"Sellout," I said.

"What?"

"You're a fucking sellout."

A fist. A face. Darkness.

PANCHO AND I were inside a cavernous warehouse with the detritus of a shattered civilization. Strange, moaning, bearded men paraded around, holding papier-mâché pig's heads on six-foot-high flaming sticks. Several black-clad teenagers, their faces covered with bandanas, had chained themselves to tall, realistic-looking plastic redwoods.

"What are you doing?" I said.

"We are practicing," said one, "for when the time comes to set the trees free."

One of the bearded men gestured me over.

"Everyone will know her name, because the snake is in her heart," he said. "And she's angry. Sometimes she can't help herself. She doesn't want to be bad, but she is. What will people say about her some day? Was she good? Was she wise? Did she tip at least 20 percent?"

"Who?" I said.

"Our head action elf," he said. "She waits for you."

His men formed a circle around him.

"To the city, gentlemen!" he shouted. "Today the system falls!"

Before me towered a monumental throne of recycled wood

pulp, which had been constructed by workers from a cooperative in Bali who receive fair compensation for their labor from a communal fund administered by an international aid agency. On the chair was a woman, splashing water on herself from a wooden bucket. Her face was painted with green-black camouflage, her hair covered in bark and leaves. But I would have recognized that T-shirt anywhere.

"Welcome to Seattle," she said.

Kim!

"I knew you'd come," she said. "I knew you were coming before you did. I could smell you from four hundred miles away. I have always had a keen sense of smell. It wasn't so long ago that I lived in Brooklyn. Chipotle was a regular feature of my diet, and I lounged aimlessly on Soho divans, listening to acid jazz and kicking my pumps into the faces of my many lovers. But then I realized how perfect it all was. I was smarter than everyone around me, and I could destroy them, devour them because they were stupid, and small, and lacked the will to change."

"I will do anything for you!" Pancho said.

"I need you in the streets," Kim said, "because the streets belong to us."

My God. She was mad. I couldn't follow her. And anyway, it looked like I wasn't going to get laid.

I MARCHED IN a phalanx because Pancho wanted to, and he was still carrying my wallet. On my right was a group of meat-eating botanists from Sri Lanka. On my left proudly walked the staff of the *Daily Cardinal,* a newspaper of the University of Wisconsin, all in garbage bags and Warren Christopher masks. A gusting cloud of smoke and gas surrounded us. We held up a banner that read "U.S. Out of Puerto Rico, At Least Temporarily!"

There were sirens, and a canister exploded overhead. Around me, people dropped, clutching their eyes and throats. Nearby, a group of rioters had overturned a gardenia planter and were claiming it as their own. There seemed to be no law. I was terribly bored and scared at the same time, and I just wanted to go home and eat a spicy tuna roll.

The crowd began to surge toward a Banana Republic. Inside, the employees cowered, and hid the nicest sweaters. Pancho stood at the front of the column, a true soldier.

"Join me, people!" he shouted. "Feel the redeeming rain of fire in your bones! The revolution has begun!"

He launched himself through the window, and we were enmeshed in a sea of glass and primary colors. The police were on us immediately. They swung batons and fired knockout darts. The smell of burning denim filled the room. I avoided trouble by shouting, "I'm a cop! I'm a cop!"

Somehow, I survived the battle without a wound, and without being arrested. Pancho lay insensate and bleeding in a corner.

"Tell me I didn't die for nothing," he said.

"You're not going to . . ."

But he was already gone.

Respectfully, meditatively, subtly tearful, I daubed tiny specks of blood off his forehead with the cuffs of a nice pair of khakis.

Wait, I realized. I love cuffs. Absolutely adore them. Look at all these pants! All around me, I saw clothing, lots of it, and it was free. At that moment, more than anything, I wanted a nice pair of olive linens, no pleats, just totally butt-hugging, with maybe a Kenneth Cole suit jacket and a tight silk T-shirt. Mmmm. I would be fit to shit. I'm telling you.

I removed my suitcase from Pancho's lifeless back, and began stuffing. I didn't stop until it brimmed, and then I filled my arms.

"Oh, Pancho," I shouted, "your death was not in vain!"

As the world splintered around me in revolution, I walked well dressed into the chaotic night.

(From *Hell Here on Earth,* Volume II, 1969)

SECRETS OF THE
MYSTERY JEW

In a nondescript trailer near the suburb of Boone, some ten miles north of Omaha, Nebraska, lives a thick-set, bearded African-American man who covers his hair with a wide-brimmed black hat, revealing only two corkscrew-shaped ringlets that snake down his face, nearly touching the tallis he never removes. According to his passport, this man is Curtis Walker, a native of the south side of Chicago, born on March 14, 1954. But the man says that he remembers himself to be somebody else—a Talmudic scholar with three Ph.D.'s, born in Crown Heights, Brooklyn— and that he regards his other identity as a farce perpetrated against him by a cruel and testy god. "We all must face our burning bush," he told me as we ate a kosher meal the other week. So his passport lists, as a second name, what he claims as his true identity: The Mystery Jew.

Four years ago, as the Mystery Jew, he published an op-ed in the *New York Times* called "James Brown: Talmud Don't Make No Mess," providing evidence that the Godfather drew from ancient literary sources while giving birth to the funk. There quickly followed two scholarly books, which Talmudic experts hailed as among the most brilliant ever written: *The Fathership Connection: Abraham in the Chocolate City* and *Elijah: Pimp Daddy of the Nile,* as well as *Satchmo's Gift,* a deeply moving novel about black Jews in

New Orleans at the turn of the century. It was a Jewish literary output unseen in the United States since Philip Roth had gotten hot. The Mystery Jew was held in awe for his ability to evoke black culture through a Jewish lens, or vice versa. Cornel West, the literary critic, declared, "At last, someone who expresses what Michael Lerner and I were trying to say a few years ago in that lame book that nobody read, you remember, the one with that picture of us on the cover shaking hands." Garry Wills, in the *New York Review of Books,* wrote as though he were describing a lost Henny Youngman monologue when he said of *Satchmo's Gift:* "It is so good, I wonder if I'm even worthy of reading it."

The Mystery Jew has since won a *Jewish Quarterly* Literary Prize in London and the Prix Baudelaire de Chien Andalou in Paris. One night, Elie Weisel even cooked him dinner, and it was delicious.

Of course, there's no way in hell this guy's really Jewish.

IT IS DIFFICULT for a Jew who has visited Jerusalem to describe to a Jew who hasn't visited Jerusalem what it is like to be a Jew in Jerusalem; the experience is that complete, that Jewish, that overwhelming. But I am not here in Jerusalem to wail at some wall, to trudge through some ancient temple, to taunt a Palestinian grandmother. I am here for a higher purpose. I am here to find out about the Mystery Jew.

My first stop is the home of the Israeli writer Aharon Appelfeld, author of *The Hebraic Negro,* a novel that he has not yet written. In a previous article I published about him for a major American magazine, Appelfeld recounted a conversation he'd had with Bernard Malamud at Wimbledon, in which Appelfeld told of meeting a virtually uneducated black man from Detroit "who had, nevertheless, an extraordinary knowledge of Jewish folklore," and "claimed to be the stepson of Golda Meir."

On a warm spring afternoon, as thousands of nameless Jews went about their business in the crowded streets outside, I sat in Appelfeld's office and prepared for a long conversation.

"Is the Mystery Jew really Jewish?" I asked.

Appelfeld fingered his beard. He flipped through a manuscript on his desk. He took a bite out of a whole grapefruit, skin on.

"I do not know," he said.

I was not prepared for this answer.

"Oh," I said. "Oh shit."

"Do you have any further questions? I have a busy day ahead."

I studied my notes carefully.

I said: "Do you have Amos Oz's phone number?"

THE MYSTERY JEW is a grumpy man, given to performing sudden imitations of obscure television dance-party hosts, such as Adrian Zmed, and prone to long spells of deafening silence: he eats a lot of pretzels; he sometimes walks backward; everything about him makes you wonder if he is a robot, or maybe a very sophisticated puppet.

Yet when it comes to Judaism, the man who claims not to be Curtis Walker, from the south side of Chicago, is a maniac. We spent a recent afternoon polishing menorahs in his trailer. He asked me if I wanted to wear an eye patch. I told him I was not a follower of Moshe Dayan, and he seemed disappointed.

The trailer is decorated simply, but Jewishly. An Israeli flag takes up one wall, a large velvet portrait of Sammy Davis Jr. much of the other. Over the Mystery Jew's bed is a hand-scrawled quote from the work of Moses Maimonides. "A man must never take a haircut on the Sabbath," it reads, "unless the Sabbath falls on a Sunday, which it never does."

"I will prove that quote wrong if it kills you," says the Mystery Jew. "Whoops. I mean me. Ha ha ha. If it kills me. Heh."

A back room of the Mystery Jew's trailer is taken up entirely with obscure documents from the annals of Hebraica: filing cabinets full of mimeographs and postcards, boxes stuffed with old hot-dog buns from Coney Island, a crate of Jackie Mason's toupees. A video monitor plays a Yitzhak Perelman concert in an endless, soundless, haunting loop.

The Mystery Jew says, warily, that people have described this trailer as a "living repository of useless Jewish crap." But he speaks of his collection as though it were a litter of precious kittens.

"How do you know I'm not Jewish?" he says. "You may think this stuff doesn't connect, but it does. It is the Nile Delta of Jewish thought. I have a photograph of Joan Rivers coming out of high-holiday services. I have all the tefillin that were worn at Henry Kissinger's bar mitzvah. I even, to my great regret, own every novel written by Leon Uris. You think that so-called great scholar Rabbi Ben Elixir of Bezalel ever had stuff like this in his files? No way!"

His hand swipes the air, as though he is fingering a secret latke.

"Am I Jewish?" he asks. "Do I make this stuff up? You tell me."

DOROTHY WALKER LIVES alone in a three-bedroom apartment on the top floor of a two-flat in a stultifying middle-class Chicago neighborhood. She is, by all accounts, the mother of the Mystery Jew, even while he continues to claim that his mother is one Shaina Mendlebaum, of Mott Street.

Dorothy sighs as she dusts her living-room portraits of Martin Luther King Jr., Malcolm X, Harold Washington, and Nipsey Russell. The pictures are identical to the ones that seem to adorn the walls of so many black people in Chicago. At least the three who I know.

Curtis was a normal boy once, Dorothy says, rubbing her tired feet with sandpaper. Like so many other kids on the block, he was seduced by the fiery rhetoric of the Black Panthers in the sixties. He sported a tall Afro, listened to the later, groovier records of Marvin Gaye, and dreamed that one day, he would run a federally funded jobs program of his own.

Then everything changed one hot summer day in 1968, as Curtis and his father, Curtis Walker Sr., were walking through the neighborhood, passing out leaflets and empowering the people. Without once honking, a bus barreled down the street and ran Curtis Sr. over, killing him instantly. The bus was full of Hasidim, who were on their way to a White Sox game.

Curtis's subsequent reaction puzzled everyone he knew.

"Curtis never cried for his father," Dorothy Walker says. "It was very strange. Instead, he just gradually became Jewish."

He put a poster of Goldie Hawn up in his bedroom. Then he started listening to Allan Sherman records. Before long, he was wearing a yarmulke to school. On Friday nights, as he and his friends would drink beer and drive around the neighborhood, Curtis took time to say a blessing over every precious can.

"I don't understand it," Dorothy says. "We raised Curtis a good Baptist and tried to teach him right from wrong. But now when he comes home for the holidays, he won't even eat my ham, shrimp, and cheese sandwiches anymore."

I feel sorry for this lonely woman who doesn't understand why her son can't mix milk with meat. My eyes fill with tears as I tell Dorothy Walker I have to leave now, to go give a lecture at the University of Chicago law school.

"Wait," she says. "Can you answer one question for me?"

"Anything," I say.

"What in the world is gefilte fish?"

"Dorothy," I say, "I wish I could tell you. But that's a question to which even a real Jew doesn't know the answer."

A FEW DAYS later, I return to Nebraska for a final nosh with the Mystery Jew. There are some questions I still want to ask him about the line between reality and fiction, truth and fantasy, truth and reality, fiction and fantasy, and other things as well. I want to tell him that I understand. Being Jewish is deeply mystifying, an impossible challenge in an oversimplified, media-hungry world, particularly when you're not Jewish.

He tells me that there's someplace special he wants us to visit together. I gladly consent, as his trailer smells of beets. We walk twenty minutes down a dirt road, farther and farther away from the main highway, past dozens of identical vinyl-sided houses, until at last we come to a field, in the center of which sits a large shed.

"What is this?" I ask.

"You'll see," he says.

Then I notice that he appears to be holding a hoelike object over his head. Wait, I realize, that is a hoe. How odd.

When I awake, I am inside the shed. It could be another shed, I suppose, but I doubt it. The Mystery Jew stands over me, his tallis twisted around him like a shroud.

"I have fooled you, like all the others," he says.

"What others?"

I feel a pounding in the back of my head, but when I move my hand to soothe the pain, I realize that the back of my head no longer exists. It has been sliced away by the hoe of the Mystery Jew. Though I feel like shrieking, I look around the shed instead. Three other men, and one woman, are chained to the wall, moaning, naked, and desperate.

Hey, I know these people! That's Mickey Kaus, formerly of *The New Republic*! And that woman peering at my notebook is Ruth Shalit! Oh no, Adam Gopnik. The Mystery Jew got him, too! And that fourth guy, the older one . . . I recognize him from somewhere.

"My God, it's Amos Oz!" I shout. "No wonder you didn't return my calls!"

"Unnnnnngh," he groans. "Arrrrrgh."

Then I realize what's really going on. All five of us are accomplished Jewish writers; all five of us have come to interview the Mystery Jew; and all five of us have succumbed to his weird plot to avenge his father's death.

"You'll never get away with this!" croaks Kaus.

"Of course I will," he says. "No one's going to miss you people. Back where you come from, there are dozens, hundreds, of ambitious journalists. And they're all eventually going to want to get to know the Mystery Jew. Soon four bodies will become six, and six ten, and ten twenty."

"And then what, Mystery Jew?" I say. "Then what?"

As he exits the shed, closing the door behind him, he says, "Then I'll write another novel, maybe something about W. E. B. DuBois on the Lower East Side. And they'll send another batch of reporters. And another . . . and another . . ."

As I begin to lose consciousness, I realize that I may never win that third National Magazine Award. After more than six months of following what I thought was the whimsical trail of a harmless eccentric, I instead lay bleeding to death in an obscure Nebraska barn with four of my colleagues, who aren't nearly as accomplished as I. The fear of what eternity holds, combined with my depression that such a great story had to turn out this way, makes me angry, very angry. This age in which we live is so trivial, so false, so vague, so decked out in stolen memories and borrowed clothes, that it's almost inevitable that writers, whoever they think they are, will also turn out to be serial killers. Life is a desperate, ungenerous fantasy, a tortured trial of secondhand opportunities and fleeting myths. Heed my sorrowful warning: The Mystery Jew wants to kill you.

He certainly has killed me.

(From *Secrets of the Mystery Jew,* 1988)

CODA:
A REVIEW OF MY
CONTEMPORARIES

The inevitable Reaper did not claim me that day in Nebraska. As everyone is now aware, the editors of *The New Republic* staged a commando raid at dawn and rescued us all from the brink. If I had died, I realize that vast mourning would have consumed the nation. But my work still would have endured, because my star in the constellation of American literary history had already been fixed, and centrally. Nonetheless, I saw my escape from the clutches of the Mystery Jew as a signal from the gods. America was transforming, and our scribes were ill equipped for the task. Except for me. The world remained my purview, and I its undeserving songmaster.

As I put the final flourishes on this volume of volumes, I realized how long I have sat atop the Olympus of American literary life, and how weak my competition has been. For instance, take this excerpt from my 1970 collection *Books Without Purpose: The New American Letters:* "We who live today are a neutered people, stumbling through the wilderness of our popular culture without any awareness of who we are or how we got there. And our writers do nothing to guide us, or to reflect on our dilemmas. Look at the authors who, today, are considered 'literary': on the one hand, you have Truman Capote, a wretched grandmamma's boy who refuses to see the world beyond the edge of his pill-soaked martini glass. On the other, there is John Barth, whose work smells musty and dated even as it is hailed by the popular press as revolutionary and avant-garde. He has as little chance of surviving the decade with his reputation intact as does that hack artist Andy Warhol, he of the hip loft and wild parties, or Bob Dylan, who inches closer to self-parody with every song. Does anyone even try to capture America as it truly is anymore, besides me? I don't think so."

In those days I was still youngish, bitter, and reeling from my first two divorces. But even now, at this pathetic, pale, tabescent moment in the history of American literature, no one stood apart. I decided that American writers, those hacks in exalted disguise, needed to be, as the youth say, "bitch slapped."

Early in 1999, I sent out an invitation for an elaborate New Year's Eve party at my Malta estate. The writers would all come, this much I knew. So rarely do I share my spoils with them that they could hardly refuse. My parties end all parties, and my predictions were soon realized; all the RSVPs came back positive, with the exception of Toni Morrison's. But I was glad for that, since my heart was still soft for her from our passionate two-year affair.

So, then, precisely at 9 P.M. on December 31, 1999, they gathered around my feast-table. To my right sat John Updike, Robert Stone, Joan Didion and John Gregory Dunne, Russell Banks, Philip Roth, and Tom Wolfe, that madman in his mauve gloves. On the other side sat the overrated Gore Vidal, Norman Mailer, George Plimpton, Susan Sontag, Hunter S. Thompson, John Irving, and, just because I wanted a piece of him, Salman Rushdie. Thomas Pynchon was at a separate table for two, with Don DeLillo, and across the table from me, in the queen's chair, was Joyce Carol Oates, reading her latest book, a fictional biography of Anne Sexton written from the point of view of Joe DiMaggio.

"Tell us what this is all about, Pollack," said the always-nosy Pynchon.

"In due time," I said. "But first, bring on the quail!"

Oh, how we dined, on skate and lamb and chanterelles. We drank whiskey and wine and Calvados by the bottle. My constitution was strong, and I felt blissfully alive. The clock ticked inexorably toward the turn of ages and my fellow scribes roared with the joy of the feast. Banks began looking a little queasy, and Thompson was stabbing at the table with a knife. I knew it was time for the sorbet.

At five minutes to midnight, I told my servants to lock the doors, except the one to the mirrored hall. To each of my guests, I handed a pair of boxing gloves and a set of fighting togs. I bid them strip down.

"You're not getting me to do this!" Irving said.

"Come on, Irving, you pussy!" Mailer shouted.

"Let's kick this guy's keister!" roared Roth.

Everyone else was blistering drunk and didn't seem to mind the prospect of a battle royal to determine who was, in fact, the greatest living American writer. As the doors opened onto the great hall, my contemporaries were shocked to see that I had placed some of the leading citizens of our time on bleachers, specially built with stadium seating. They were all there—bankers, lawyers, doctors, politicians, heads of Internet commerce, and even some bold religious leaders. They quivered with excitement as we authors huddled together, tipsy as hell, our bodies soaked in anticipatory sweat.

My servants placed blindfolds on us, and Updike began to weep. The blindfold was tight and I felt a lessening of blood flow to my brain. I heard the bell clang, the opening notes of Tchaikovsky's Violin Concerto in D, and a scuffling of feet. I smacked my lips in anticipation of the hide-whupping I was about to deliver.

A glove slammed into my rib cage, but my stomach of steel deflected the blow with ease. From across the room, I heard a telltale, "Ooooooooooooh! My eye!" and I knew that someone had felled Rushdie.

Blows pounded on me from all sides, but I was landing death

185

punches, my senses honed from a dozen years of upper-level tai chi. The air was splattered with sweat and blood. The salty-sweet odor of urine emanated from a far corner. I swung up and down, connecting and not connecting. The grunting and moaning grew, and then ceased, and then swelled again. Someone clobbered my face, and my mouth filled with unholy blood.

"Bastards!" I screamed, and I tore through the ranks like a hyper-aware crab with claws of steel, achieving ultimate smack-down.

My blindfold slipped off. Only four of us remained conscious. Thompson and Stone were going at it in a far corner, and Hunter S. appeared to have the upper hand. Stone punched the air and rarely landed an uppercut, while Thompson stayed below the belt, as is his wont. Finally, he landed a sucker punch, and Stone dropped like a rock. Thompson threw his hands in the air exultantly. Then he smacked himself in the jaw and he, too, was gone.

Across the room lurked the colossus himself. He climbed over the near-lifeless form of Joyce Carol Oates and strode past the pulpy mess that had once been George Plimpton, the Paper Lion.

His blindfold, too, had fallen away, and he faced me, his eyes aflame.

"Are you ready for me, Pollack?" he said.

"Bring it, Mailer," I said. "Give me your best shot."

He launched himself at me like a jackal that had skipped breakfast. He grabbed my shoulders. I slipped in a pool of blood and saliva, momentarily dazed by the swirl of lights and smoke and laughter.

Mailer threw punches and kicked at my groin. I struggled, feeling, for the first time in my literary career, true, pure terror. My arms were leaden, my legs unhelpful.

"Die forever in hell!" said my eternal adversary.

"Four hundred dollars on Mailer!" I heard from the crowd.

I pushed him away and staggered upright, but I knew, as the stocky brute advanced on me, that these would be my last moments at the top of the charts.

Wait! What was that hovering above? The still-robust ghost of my one true love Wally Trumbull gestured to me from some blue distance, and I heard his stalwart Spartan beauty singing my name from beyond the stars. Suddenly I knew my final destiny. I would write until I died because the final game of rough-and-tumble awaited me in Elysium, where Wally stood, hands on Herculean hips, laughing, potent, and forever warm to my touch.

"Oh, Wally!" I shouted.

Mailer looked stunned.

"Who the hell are you talking to?" he said.

The Wally-spirit laughed above, and I could sense his animative celestial inspiration filling me with all the strength of irresistible, eternal youth. Wally awaited me in his cosseted heaven, but there was so much for me yet to accomplish.

"You're mine, Norm!" I said.

Wally's essence flowed through my arms and I unleashed a roundhouse onto Mailer's pudgy chin.

He stood, but only out of habit.

"You win, Pollack," he moaned, and collapsed onto the parquet.

The crowd roared insanely. I had won them completely. I had given them something they had never seen before. My contemporaries surrounded me, insensate, unconscious, and bloody, and I knew then, as I know now, that I was truly the greatest writer in the world.

BREAKING NEWS: ONE
AGAINST THE TALIBAN

SEPTEMBER 11, 2001
NEW YORK CITY

Enough time has now passed so I'm no longer ashamed to admit that at the last moment of the old ways, I was sitting at my desk in my Brooklyn loft, preparing to write an article about the rise in popularity of the Latin Grammys. At 8:50 A.M., the phone rang. It was a fashion editor with whom I'd slept two nights earlier.

"You'd better go up on your roof," she said, "and bring a notebook."

We all know what the next four hours were like, and my experiences did not diverge from those of other published writers. I felt a mixture of grief, fear, anger, and revulsion, along with hope that the *Times Magazine* might call for my contribution to the special issue that would inevitably emerge from this chaos. After the second tower fell, I composed a metaphor in my head that went, "the World Trade Center was our remembrance of *temps perdu,* and when it collapsed, like two cakes in an overwarm oven . . ."

Reading those sentences now, in retrospect, I'm encouraged by my wit and sensitivity under such extreme conditions. Because in times of grief and trouble, the arts must rise, and writers must write about the rise of the arts, for pages and pages, with references to Orwell and true satire in the Brechtian sense. I, as a three-time winner of the National Book Award and seventeen-time selectee for *The Best American Short Stories,* can prove no exception to the immutable rules of redemptive prose.

On that day, after a brief scroll through my Palm VI to ensure that all my editors worked in midtown, I went for a walk in my neighborhood among the ordinary people, with their anguished, confused faces. I collected several oral histories en route, and the raw human narrative, that vein of gold that runs through all New York's noble, hardworking residents, broke my heart. But I was encouraged that I hadn't lost my essential reporting skills. Through many national calamities—the Kennedy assassination, the My Lai massacre, the 1968 Democratic National Convention, Kent State, the unexpected cancellation of *The Beverly Hillbillies,* Watergate, Broadway versions of Disney cartoon musicals, Waco, the deaths of Princess Diana and JFK Jr., Columbine, and beyond—the American people have shown astonishing resilience in the face of lost innocence. And I have been there to chronicle their sad journey of courage.

I returned home to find five hundred messages on my answering machine. All three of my E-mail accounts were brimming. Mostly, I'd heard from famous, important, wonderful people, including several published novelists, informing me that they were OK. There were also already several requests to participate in benefit readings. But one message stood out among the rest:

> HI. THIS IS Jenny. I don't know if you remember me, but I'm an assistant art director. I met you at a party a couple of weeks ago, and we made out in the stairwell. Anyway, I live on Flatbush Avenue, and my room-mates are out of town, and I'm scared, lonely, and kind of horny. We don't know each other well, but could you please come over?

It was the least I could do in this time of crisis.

Several ecstatic, desperate, loving hours later, I returned to my Brooklyn loft with its now tragic view of lower Manhattan. I was spent and exhausted. America would never be the same, I thought. Yet it was, to me, curiously the same, except for my sex life, which I'd previously thought could never improve.

I began work, because work was all I had. I wrote one piece arguing that we should suspend all civil liberties and personal freedoms until the "scourge of terrorism is wiped forever from our shores," and another that said "we, the evilest and most self-deluding of all empires, had it coming, and man, did we take it smack in the kisser." I also started writing about the end of satire, which is imminent, and about how if my teenage daughter wanted to fly the flag from her bedroom window I wouldn't let her because patriotism is blind and stupid. Then I remembered that I didn't have a teenage daughter and began to weep for the years I'd lost.

My misery was interrupted by a phone call from the editor in chief of the best-paying American magazine.

"The age of irony is over," he said. "We're sending you to Pakistan."

September 20, 2001
Peshawar, Pakistan

It was 1979, or maybe 1981. Across the floodplain, the ground was tinted blue against the setting of the pinkish-orange sky. Our truck, parked behind a mound of hilly dirt, seemed pointless in a landscape of irregular rocks, mortar shells, and broken bones. I looked at the tired, hungry, heat-worn faces of the mujahedeen around me, and even then I knew that when this war was over—and it would be over, if I had to spend ten years and 20,000 words in Afghanistan chronicling it—these soldiers would become hard-line religious fanatics who would threaten the very foundations of civilization itself. They placed a Kalashnikov in my hairy, muscular arms and bid me fire upon the Soviets. I shot the rocket, with its red glare, sad in the knowledge that one empire would only replace another, because I have seen the evil that men do.

I was there in 1973, when King Zahir Shah was overthrown by his cousin. I was there in 1979, when President Taraki was murdered by his deputy. In fact, I was there when secret CIA operatives planned that murder, which I wrote about at length in my Caldecott Medal–winning children's book *A Hot Boiling Lie: The CIA-Sponsored Murder of President Taraki.* I witnessed, on and off, the entire Soviet-Afghan War and was the only American reporter present at the siege of Jalalabad. As recently as June of this year, I was among the Northern Alliance, working on the last really good prose piece about Ahmad Shah Massoud, whom I described as "a rebellious dog barking into the gorge of terror." I still remember the last thing he said to me before I left on a much-needed vacation to Maine.

"We are lonely," he said. "Please send us female exchange students—from Switzerland."

Now I've returned to this most troubled of regions, too soon, sadly, too soon, but with a bigger budget than I've had in years. That great postmillennial war reportorial circus bazaar is going full bore. Let's get it on, as Marvin sang so many years ago.

The only bar in Peshawar is full of white people in brown jackets, looking for something to do. I sit next to a woman with close-cut brown hair, serious-looking glasses, and not too much makeup. She's wearing a nametag that reads: "HELLO. My name is ASHLEIGH."

"Hey," I say.

"Omigod!" she says. "Are you an American? Because I totally am!"

"Yes," I say, "though I consider myself more of a global citizen."

"Really?" she says, removing her glasses and chewing on them thoughtfully. "That's cool! I work for NBC!"

"NBC News?"

"Yes," she says. "Isn't that *awesome*!" Then she adds, "I hear they're calling this Operation Get O.B.L. You know what O.B.L. stands for?"

"No."

She looks at me sternly, like I am a camera, or an audience of millions.

"Osama bin Laden. And the State Department says he is the prime target."

I am aware of Osama bin Laden. Painfully aware. I've interviewed him several times over the last five years, and have warned Americans about him since the beginning, particularly in my *Atlantic Monthly* article from October 1998, "Osama bin Laden's Al Qaeda Network: The Greatest Threat to Peace and Stability the World Has Ever Known." Yet for some reason, the talk shows ignored me on that one.

"Hey!" Ashleigh says. "Did you know I used to be blond?"

"It doesn't surprise me."

"Last time I was in the Middle East, I got majorly harassed. It sucked. But now I'm a brunette."

"I see."

"And I'm getting married! To a producer! Isn't that cool?"

A loud noise erupts outside. Through the streets swarm hundreds, maybe thousands of men. They're shouting anti-U.S. slogans, in pretty good English, actually. Ashleigh and I spring up, leaving our gin and tonics half consumed.

"Lou!" she shouts to a heavy man sleeping in the corner. "Get off your Teamster ass and start filming this shit!"

"I'm not a Teamster!" he says.

"Whatever," she says. "All unions are the same!"

We rush into the street, where the mob burns an effigy of Carson Daly. "It appears," I write frantically, "that the purveyors of the global entertainment state have found themselves pilloried on a roost of fire."

Then I hear, "Down with the Satanist Western media hordes!"

I find myself running down an alley with Dr. Bob Arnot. What is *he* doing here, anyway? We trip over beggar children in the street, but I don't have time for these Third World types right now, and soon we are in a central square, surrounded by men with torches and guns. I think about how fortunate I am to once again be a witness to history. A rock hits Ashleigh square in her glasses, which shatter.

"Bastards!" she shouts, as she pulls an identical pair from her stylish reporter's vest.

LINE DELETED HERE.

Then comes the bullhorned plea: "Wait! We must spare them!"

"Why?" the crowd shouts in unison.

"Don't you know?" asks the voice of reason. "You cannot kill him! For he is the greatest living American author!"

I knew that writing a book called *The Secret Pleasures of Fundamentalism* would come in handy someday.

SEPTEMBER 27, 2001
KABUL, AFGHANISTAN

I arrive in the center of Kabul near dusk. A veil of cool horror swims through the air as the Taliban obey their call to evening prayer. The driver stops my car to join them, which gives me time to collect my thoughts in a notebook. This is my first visit to Kabul since 1990. I see that my favorite old hotel, the British Empire Arms, has burned down, replaced by mere crisp shards of rubble in the cruel night. Also, the famed Afghan strip malls, which once boasted some of the worlds largest Banana Republics, now contain only three types of stores: Switch World, Burqaland, and I Can't Believe We Like to Skin Our Enemies Alive! It is also apparent that everywhere, the Taliban are uprooting trees. I spy an ominous billboard that reads, "Trees Are a Crime Against Nature." My body shudders preternaturally, though that may be because my own particular brand of barbiturates has been banned here as well.

After prayers, my guide drives me through the rubble of Kabul, while the Taliban skip arm-in-arm, singing their merry little song:

We are the Taliban
The Taliban are we!
We like to beat up women
And we like to drink our tea!
If we give them enough heroin
Our enemies will flee!
La-di-da-di-da-di-doo
La-di-da-di-da-di-di!
We are the Taliban!
The Taliban are we!

My guide says to me, "We are attempting to forbid all speech in this country, except by members of the Taliban."

"How?" I ask.

"Quiet, infidel!" he shouts, and slaps me across the head.

"Oh," I say, and he slaps me again.

He stops the car and tells me to get out. Someone grabs my arms and someone else blindfolds me. I can't see, which I guess is what they intended. Then they spin me around a few times until I'm kind of dizzy. They march me forward, and up some stairs, and down some other stairs, and then they make me swim across what I hope is a pool, and then we walk down a long corridor.

When they remove my blindfold, I'm facing a forty-one-year-old man with one eye.

"How's it going?" I ask.

"Pretty good," he says. "Did you lose anyone in the attacks?"

"No, thank God," I say.

"What a shame," he replies. "For we want all Americans to live in misery and fear!"

"Oh," I say. "Can I quote you on that?"

"Yes," he says. "I am the commander of the faithful, the supreme leader of the Taliban. My name is Mohammed Omar, and I have chosen you to spread my message to the American people."

NOTE: SEVERAL LINES DELETED HERE.

Sixteen hours pass before he finishes his stupid message. I

keep trying to fall asleep, but every time I nod, he slaps me upside the head.

"Where," I moan, "is Osama bin Laden?"

"We don't know," says Mohammed Omar.

"Yes," I say, "you do."

I feel myself teetering toward insanity.

"Do!" I shout.

"Don't!"

"Do! Do! Do! Do! Do!"

"Oh, all right already," says the commander of the faithful.

He pulls aside a curtain. Behind it sits a bearded, turbaned, sandaled man who holds a machine gun in his lap.

"No . . ." I croak.

"Pleased to meet you," says the man. "Hope you guessed my name."

SEPTEMBER 28, 2001
SOME CAVE IN AFGHANISTAN

Osama bin Laden and I spend several hours together, just catching up. We have so much in common. Like me, he is from a wealthy family and had the finest education. We both fought as insurgent rebels in the 1980s, he against the Soviets in Afghanistan, me as a Special Forces commando in Guatemala. We both share a love for the work of Denzel Washington, going all the way back to *St. Elsewhere.* And over the years we both gradually developed a distrust of the United States and its foreign policies. I suppose that's where the similarity ends, though, because I took my doubts and became a regular on the liberal-arts-college speaking circuit, while he became the murderous enemy of all things decent on the earth.

Our conversation takes a bitter turn.

"You're a scumbag," I say to him.

"Ha-hah!" he says. "What do *you* know?"

He reaches into his robe and pulls out something unexpected.

"Perhaps now you would like to be entertained by Jimmy the Jihad Chicken," he says.

The surprising chicken does a hideous strut as Osama begins to sing, clapping his hands merrily:

Oh, I wish I was back in old Medina
With twenty wives sucking on my weina.
Look away!
Look away!
Look away!
Holy land.
I wish I was in Mecca.
Hooray!
Hooray!
The Saudis better have a plan
To live or die in Mecca.
Away,
Away,
No gays down south
In Mecca!

God, what an awful song. In America, it would probably be considered racist. I wonder who the hell wrote it.

"This is not entertainment!" I say. " It's just the desperate act of a man who's out of funny ideas!"

He says, "As opposed to most American entertainment, including the sketches at the Gridiron Club dinner?"

I realize that our empire is built on fragile hypocrisies. In fact, I've pointed them out repeatedly through the decades, first in *Our Man In Tarzana,* my novel about the military-industrial complex, and subsequently in the speeches I wrote for Ralph Nader's nearly successful 2000 presidential bid. My online column regularly attacks the banalities of contemporary television and music. But I don't want to hear about them now, particularly not from Osama bin Laden and his goddamn dancing chicken. With my exclusive access, I'm going to do the job that no one else can. I am a star-spangled avenger, and I am going to kick Osama bin Laden's ass!

"For all the world," I shout, "I condemn you to die!"

I bolt from my chair. With a patriotic hammer-blow, I knock the gun from his hands.

He grabs hold of my neck. I respond with a knee to his groin. Jimmy the Jihad Chicken pecks away at my leg. But Osama can barely lay a hand on my body, which, after all, ripples from years of amateur kickboxing. My fists land blows on his face and his torso. His beard cannot cushion them all.

I reach around me, grab a conveniently placed stone, and bring it down toward his head.

"Objectivity be damned!" I shout.

"Look!" says Osama bin Laden, pointing behind me. "The Pulitzer selection committee is coming!"

I turn around.

"Where?" I say. "Where?"

Quickly, I realize that he's attempted an evasive measure, and I whip back to resume my smashing. But the rock connects with empty ground.

Damnit! I can still feel his hot, genocidal breath on my neck! I had the bastard!

In the distance, I hear his signature villain's laugh: "Mwah-ha-ha-ha-ha-ha-ha-ha!"

Killing him, I realize, would have brought me an advance bigger than Clinton's, and I weep, for democracy and for my career. But I can still gain some manner of vengeance.

I stare into the face of Jimmy the Jihad Chicken and think, *fricassee*.

NOVEMBER 7, 2001
SOME OTHER, FRIENDLIER CAVE IN AFGHANISTAN

As I conclude this dispatch, many miles away from unsafe Taliban-infested harbors, great waves of war crash onto the shores of the world, and I encourage America to stay strong like me. Once again I find myself cradled in the company of my beloved Northern Alliance, who mercifully have been feeding me Stouffer's Double Cheese French Bread Pizza. This food is otherwise forbidden in Afghanistan, but we are eating heartily now, courtesy of the United States's well-thought-out and highly effective strategy of dropping humanitarian aid packages into random mountain locations.

By the time you read this, we may already have caught Osama bin Laden. As the great apocalyptic prophet Barry McCaffrey has predicted, the evil Taliban regime may already have crumbled, in the deep of night, with no witnesses around. A new generation of American heroes may have been forged in the fires of battle and photographed by the chroniclers of the fires of battle. I may, in fact, already be home talking about the war on *Hardball*. It's inevitable that since I wrote this feeble line, the world has changed violently. But I want you, my readers, to take solace. Because whatever happened, wherever in the world, I was there.

In the distance, I can hear the bombs, and it is time for bed. Come morning, the battle begins anew. With one of the top-ten fighting forces in the world forming a phalanx around me, I am ready to return to the scrum.

I blow out the candle that is my only friend and shout to the far mountains, proud to use a cliché for the first time in my long life, "I'll get you, Osama bin Laden, wherever you are!"

STUDY GUIDE

ABOUT THIS GUIDE

The questions, discussion topics, and author biography that follow are designed to enhance, if such a thing were possible, your group's reading and discussion of Neal Pollack's masterwork, *The Neal Pollack Anthology of American Literature.* We hope they provide you with a starting point for the soul-searching experience you are about to undertake. In these times of national crisis, with increased arsenic in the drinking water, do not come to shallow, hasty conclusions about this book. It is a work of art that necessitates careful thought, and maybe even a weekend retreat.

INTRODUCTION

Neal Pollack has been the Greatest Living American Writer across six decades, seven continents, and ten wives. He has won the Pulitzer Prize, the Booker Prize, the PEN/Faulkner Award (twice), and the Premio Simón Bolívar for contributions to the people's struggle in Latin America. In 1985, Pollack's writing was declared "beyond our standards" by the Swedish Academy. With the publication of *The Neal Pollack Anthology of American Literature,* the definitive collection of his work in English, a new generation is set to immerse itself in Pollack's magic ink. In the

Anthology, Pollack seeks to discover nothing less than the meaning of human existence on Earth. As always, he succeeds.

THIS ASTONISHING WORK of fictitious nonfiction, the funniest and most creatively styled postmodernist confection of its time, has been universally praised as the best book ever written except for maybe *Don Quixote* and *The Shipping News*. No one sees the world like Neal Pollack. Anyone would be an idiot to even try.

FOR DISCUSSION

1. Neal Pollack has been accused by his few critics, all of whom are jealous failures, of being "over-perceptive" about how the world really works. In the *Anthology*'s witty, urbane introduction, Pollack answers his critics, calling them "flaccid fuckpigs." Why might Pollack use such a praise to attack obviously lesser writers? Place his statement in a timeline of his other literary feuds. Why does he always win?

2. Early in the *Anthology,* Pollack reveals that many of the excerpts previously appeared in various magazines under other titles. Is there some law that forces him to reveal this to us? Since we know that all magazines suck, who cares?

3. In the book's opening essay, "The Albania of My Existence," Pollack points out that he had to eat "dirt for lunch" (page 1). Is Pollack's book remarkable because of the incredible empathy that he has for his characters, or because of his stylistic and narrative risks? Why is he able, like no other Western author, to understand the struggles of the world's forgotten peoples?

4. It has been noted by *Newsweek* that the major theme of the *Anthology* is the "unspoken lust that all the world's women seem to feel" for Pollack's still-ample body and razor-sharp eyes. From personal experience, it is true that Pollack's lovemaking skills are nearly beyond comprehension, and that in his pres-

ence, women are nearly always brought to weeping orgasms. Have you had sex with Neal Pollack? What was it like?

5. Is it really easy, as Pollack claims, to take a lover in Cuba? If not, why would Pollack make such a claim? Are there times when a writer, because of his superior connections and vast experience, finds certain experiences attainable that the rest of the world does not? Should we be jealous of such a person or merely live vicariously through him?

6. Pollack suffers a personal crisis in "I Am Friends with a Working-Class Black Woman," excerpted from *Leon: A Man of the Streets,* the first of a projected tetralogy of novels about the African-American experience. Does this crisis feel genuine to you? Should Pollack feel such discomfort around black people when his game is obviously tight? Would you like to "kick it" with Neal Pollack?

7. In "My Week at Sea," Pollack has spun the greatest tale of men and water ever written. But do you think a relatively privileged writer who doesn't actually have to suffer the hardships of a seafarer's life has the right to reveal, and, to some extent, shape, other people's tragic narratives, especially since those people may not appreciate seeing their lives portrayed as found art? Is such an approach exploitative? Can one accidentally glamorize the life of working people in magazine articles? Just asking.

8. Is Neal Pollack better looking than Norman Mailer? Is his prose sexier than Philip Roth's? Could he kick John Updike's WASP ass at golf? What about putt-putt golf?

9. Drugs, and drug references, play a big part in Pollack's world. Is this book better when you're stoned? If you don't know for sure, why not give it a shot? Take a big bong hit and open the *Anthology* up to any page. By the way, does anyone know where Pollack can get some horse tranquilizers? He has a long flight to Asia coming up.

10. What significance does the figure of Wally Trumbull have in the *Anthology* and in Pollack's life? Why does Wally haunt him so? Why can Pollack still remember the first time he woke up in Wally's arms, that tender morning on the Cape so long ago? Wally's legs were covered in little tufts of doe-hair, the first blush of manhood! When one has had such a love, how can any relationship compare? When will Pollack finally die so that he can join Wally in Nirvana, as the soothsayer promised?

11. Like many men of his generation, Pollack is a multimillionaire and has a home in Mustique. Have you heard about the exclusive parties that he's thrown there? Do you wish you'd been invited?

12. Did Pollack's time on the Hollywood blacklist affect his feelings about what he calls the "entertainment-industrial-chemical mind-altering" complex? Also, how has Pollack's occasional alienation from the mainstream influenced three generations of the American and European avant-garde?

13. Can you feel Pollack inside your mind when you read his books? He is there, with you, all the time. He knows your thoughts and feels your heart beating. He wants you to slide your hand into your pants and touch yourself. Everything he writes is for you. He is in your body now, and is your soul mate. He wants you to come for him. Oh, baby. He wants to fuck you so bad. Mmmm. Oh, God. He wishes he were in bed with you right now, fucking you. Feel him there beside you. Come for him. Come for him now!

FOR FURTHER READING

Henry Adams, *The Education of Henry Adams;* Albert Camus, *The Stranger;* Italo Calvino, *The Baron in the Trees;* Jackie Collins, *Lucky;* Charles Dickens, *Bleak House;* James Dickey, *Deliverance;*

Franklin W. Dixon, *The Monkey's Paw;* George Eliot, *Middlemarch;* Ralph Ellison, *Invisible Man;* Gustave Flaubert, *A Sentimental Education;* John Grisham, *The Pelican Brief;* James Joyce, *Ulysses;* Herman Melville, *Moby-Dick;* James A. Michener, *Chesapeake;* Vladimir Nabokov, *Lolita;* Thomas Pynchon, *Gravity's Rainbow;* The Rock, *The Rock Speaks;* Stendahl, *The Red and the Black;* Leo Tolstoy, *Anna Karenina;* Rebecca Wells, *Divine Secrets of the Ya-Ya Sisterhood.*